ALL THE WRONG
QUESTIONS

ALL THE WRONG QUESTIONS

"Who Could That Be at This Hour?"
"When Did You See Her Last?"

ALL THE WRONG QUESTIONS

2

"When Did You See Her Last?"

LEMONY SNICKET

ART BY SETH

Little, Brown and Company
New York Boston

Little, Brown and Company

Hachette Book Group
237 Park Avenue, New York, NY 10017
Visit our website at www.lb-kids.com

Little, Brown and Company is a division of Hachette Book Group, Inc.
The Little, Brown name and logo are trademarks of
Hachette Book Group, Inc.

The publisher is not responsible for websites (or their content)
that are not owned by the publisher.

First Edition: October 2013

Library of Congress Control Number: 2012955921

ISBN 978-0-316-12305-1

10 9 8 7 6 5 4 3 2 1

RRD-C

Printed in the United States of America

TO: Pocket
FROM: LS
FILE UNDER: Stain'd-by-the-Sea, accounts of; kidnapping,
investigations of; Hangfire; skip tracing; laudanum;
doppelgängers; et cetera
2/4
cc: VFDhq

CHAPTER ONE

There was a town, and there was a statue, and there was a person who had been kidnapped. While I was in the town, I was hired to rescue this person, and I thought the statue was gone forever. I was almost thirteen and I was wrong. I was wrong about all of it. I should have asked the question "How could someone who was missing be in two places at once?" Instead, I asked the wrong question—four wrong questions, more or less. This is the account of the second.

It was cold and it was morning and I needed a haircut. I didn't like it. When you need a haircut, it looks like you have no one to take care of you. In my case it was true. There was no one taking care of me at the Lost Arms, the hotel in which I found myself living. My room was called the Far East Suite, although it was not a suite, and I shared it with a woman who was called S. Theodora Markson, although I did not know what the S stood for. It was not a nice room, and I tried not to spend too much time in it, except when I was sleeping, trying to sleep, pretending to sleep, or eating a meal. Theodora cooked most of our meals herself, although "cooking" is too fancy a word for what she did. What she did was purchase groceries from a half-empty store a few blocks away and then warm them up on a small, heated plate that plugged into the wall. That morning breakfast was a fried egg, which Theodora had served to me on a towel from the bathroom. She kept forgetting to buy plates, although she occasionally remembered to blame me for letting her forget. Most of the egg stuck to the towel, so I didn't eat much of it, but I had managed to find an apple that wasn't too bruised and now I sat in the lobby of the Lost Arms with its sticky core in my hand. There wasn't much else in the lobby. There was a man named Prosper Lost, who ran the place with a smile that made me step back as if it were something crawling out of a drawer, and there was a phone in a small booth in the corner that was nearly always in use, and there was a plaster statue of a woman without clothes or arms. She needed a sweater, a long one without sleeves. I liked to sit beneath her on a dirty sofa and think. If you want to know the truth, I was thinking about Ellington Feint, a girl with strange, curved eyebrows like question marks, and green eyes, and a smile that might have meant anything. I had not seen that smile for some time. Ellington Feint had run off, clutching a statue in the shape of the

3

Bombinating Beast. The beast was a very terrible creature in very old myths, whom sailors and citizens were worried about encountering. All I was worried about was encountering Ellington. I did not know where she was or when I might see her again. The phone rang right on schedule.

"Hello?" I said.

There was a careful pause before she said "Good morning." "Good morning," she said. "I'm conducting a voluntary survey. 'A survey' means you'll be answering questions, and 'voluntary' means—"

"I know what voluntary means," I interrupted, as planned. "It means I'll be volunteering."

"Exactly, sir," she said. It was funny to hear my sister call me sir. "Is now a good time to answer some questions?"

"Yes, I have a few minutes," I said.

"The first question is, how many people are currently in your household?"

I looked at Prosper Lost, who was across

the room, standing at his desk and looking at his fingernails. Soon he would notice I was on the phone and find some reason to stand where he might eavesdrop better. "I live alone," I said, "but only for the time being."

"I know just what you mean." I knew from my sister's reply that she was also in a place without privacy. Lately it had not been safe to talk on the phone, and not only because of eavesdroppers. There was a man named Hangfire, a villain who had become the focus of my investigations. Hangfire had the unnerving ability to imitate anyone's voice, which meant you could not always be sure whom you were talking to on the telephone. You also couldn't be sure when Hangfire would turn up again, or what his scheme might be. It was entirely too many things to be unsure about.

"In fact," my sister continued, "things in my own household have become so complicated that I am unsure I can get to the library anymore."

"I'm sorry to hear that," I said, which was code for being sorry to hear that. Recently my sister and I had been communicating through the library system. Now she seemed to be telling me that it would no longer be possible.

"My second question is, do you prefer visiting a museum alone or with a companion?"

"With a companion," I said quickly. "Nobody should go to a museum alone."

"What if you could not find your usual companion," she asked, "because he was very far away?"

I wasted a few seconds staring at the receiver in my hand, as if I could peer through the little holes and see all the way to the city, where my sister was, like me, working as an apprentice. "Then you should find another companion," I said, "rather than visiting a museum by yourself."

"What if there were no other suitable companions?" she asked, and then her voice changed, as if someone had walked into the room. "That's my third question, sir."

"Then you should not go to the museum at all," I said, but then I, too, was interrupted, by the figure of S. Theodora Markson coming down the stairs. Her hair came first, a wild tangle as if several heads of hair were having a wrestling match, and the rest of her followed, frowning and tall. There are many mysteries I have never solved, and the hair of my chaperone is perhaps my most curious unsolved case.

"But sir—" my sister was saying, but I had to interrupt her again.

"Give Jacques my regards," I said, which was a phrase which here meant two things. One was "I must get off the phone." The other thing the phrase meant was exactly what it said.

"There you are, Snicket," Theodora said to me. "I've been looking for you everywhere. It's a missing-persons case."

"It's not a missing-persons case," I said

patiently. "I told you I was going to be in the lobby."

"Be sensible," Theodora told me. "You know I don't listen to you very well in the morning, and so you should make the proper adjustments. If you're going to be someplace in the morning, tell me in the afternoon. But where you are is neither here nor there. As of this morning, Snicket, we're skip tracers."

"Skip tracers?"

"'Skip tracer' is a term which here means 'a person who finds missing persons and brings them back.' Come on, Snicket, we're in a great hurry."

Theodora had an impressive vocabulary, which can be charming if it is used at a convenient time. But if you are in a great hurry and someone uses something like "skip tracer," which you are unlikely to understand, then an impressive vocabulary is quite irritating.

Another way of saying this is that it is vexing. Another way of saying this is that it is annoying. Another way of saying this is that it is bothersome. Another way of saying this is that it is exasperating. Another way of saying this is that it is troublesome. Another way of saying this is that it is chafing. Another way of saying this is that it is nettling. Another way of saying this is that it is ruffling. Another way of saying this is that it is infuriating or enraging or aggravating or embittering or envenoming, or that it gets one's goat or raises one's dander or makes one's blood boil or gets one hot under the collar or blue in the face or mad as a wet hen or on the warpath or in a huff or up in arms or in high dudgeon, and as you can see, it also wastes time when there isn't any time to waste. I followed Theodora out of the Lost Arms to where her dilapidated roadster was parked badly at the curb. She slid into the driver's seat and put on the leather helmet she always wore when driving, which was the primary suspect in the mystery of why her hair always looked so odd.

We were in a town called Stain'd-by-the-Sea, which was no longer by the sea and was hardly a town anymore. The streets were quiet and many buildings were empty, but here and there I could see signs of life. We passed Hungry's, a diner I had yet to try, and I saw through the window the shapes of several people having breakfast. We passed Partial Foods, where we purchased our groceries, and I saw a shopper or two walking among the half-empty shelves. Black Cat Coffee had a solitary figure at the counter, pressing one of the three automated buttons that gave customers coffee, bread, or access to the attic, which had served as a good hiding place. On this drive I also noticed something new in town— something pasted up on the sides of lampposts, and on the wood that barricaded the doors and windows of abandoned houses. Even the mailboxes had the posters on them, although from the hurrying roadster I could only read one word on them.

"This is a very crucial matter," Theodora was saying. "We were given this important case because of our earlier success with the theft of the statue of the Bombinating Beast."

"I would not call it success," I said.

"I don't care what you would call it," Theodora said. "Try to be more like your predecessor, Snicket."

I was tired of hearing about the apprentice before me. Theodora had liked him better, which made me think he was worse. "We were hired to return that statue to its rightful owners," I reminded her, "but that turned out to be one of Hangfire's tricks, and now both the item and the villain could be anywhere."

"I think you're just mooning over that girl Eleanor," Theodora said. "Cupidity is not an attractive quality in an apprentice, Snicket."

I was not sure what "cupidity" meant, but it began with the word "Cupid," the winged god of love, and Theodora was using the tone of voice everyone uses to tease boys who have friends who are girls. I felt myself blushing and did not want to say her name, which wasn't Eleanor. "She is in danger," I said instead, "and I promised to help her."

"You're not concentrating on the right person," Theodora said, and tossed a large envelope into my lap. The envelope had a black seal on it that had been broken. Inside was nothing but a piece of paper with a photograph of a girl several years older than I was. She had hair so blond it looked white and glasses that made her eyes look very small. The glasses were shiny, or maybe just reflecting the light of the camera's flash. Her clothes looked brand-new, with brand-new black-and-white stripes like a zebra that had been recently polished. She was standing in what I guessed to be her bedroom, which also looked brand-new. I could see the edge of a shiny bed and a shiny dresser stacked with trophies that looked as if they had been awarded yesterday. Most trophies I'd seen had figures of athletes at the top of them. These had shapes that were bright and strange. They reminded me of illustrations in a science book, explaining the very small things that supposedly make up the world. The only things in the photograph that did not look brand-new were the hat she was wearing, which was round and the color of a raspberry, and the frown on her face. She looked displeased at having her photograph taken, and also like she used her displeased expression quite frequently. Printed underneath the frowning girl was her name,

MISS CLEO KNIGHT, and at the top of the poster was printed another word, in much bigger type. It was the same word I had read on the copies of the same flyer all over town.

MISSING.

The word applied to the girl, but it could have applied to anything in town. Ellington Feint had vanished. Theodora's roadster sped down whole blocks that had been emptied of businesses and people. I realized we were heading toward the town's tallest building, a tower shaped like an enormous pen. Once this town had been known for producing the world's darkest ink, from frightened octopi shivering in deep wells that were once under-water. But the sea had been drained away, leaving behind an eerie, lawless expanse of sea-weed that somehow still lived even when the water had disappeared. Nowadays there were few octopi left, and eventually there would be nothing at all but the shimmering seaweed of the Clusterous Forest. Soon everything will go missing, Snicket, I thought to myself. Your chaperone is right. You are in a great hurry. If you do not hurry to find what has gone missing, there will be nothing left.

CHAPTER TWO

The pen-shaped tower had a surprisingly small door printed with letters that were far too large. The letters said INK INC., and the doorbell was in the shape of a small, dark ink stain. It was the name of the largest business in Stain'd-by-the-Sea. Theodora stuck out a gloved finger and rang the doorbell six times in a row. There was not a doorbell in the world that Theodora did not ring six times when she encountered it.

"Why do you do that?"

My chaperone drew herself up to her full height and took off her helmet so her hair could make her even taller. "S. Theodora Markson does not need to explain anything to anybody," she said.

"What does the *S* stand for?" I asked.

"Silence," she hissed, and the door opened to reveal two identical faces and a familiar scent. The faces belonged to two worried-looking women in black clothes almost completely covered in enormous white aprons, but I could not quite place the smell. It was sweet but wrong, like an evil bunch of flowers.

"Are you S. Theodora Markson?" one of the women said.

"No," Theodora said, "*I* am."

"We meant you," said the other woman.

"Oh," Theodora said. "In that case, yes. And this is my apprentice. You don't need to know his name."

I told them anyway.

"I'm Zada and this is Zora," said one of the women. "We're the Knight family servants. Don't worry about telling us apart. Miss Knight is the only one who can. You'll find her, won't you, Ms. Markson?"

"Please call me Theodora."

"We've known Miss Knight since she was a baby. We're the ones who took her home from the hospital when she was born. You'll find her, won't you, Theodora?"

"Unless you would prefer to call me Ms. Markson. It really doesn't matter to me one way or the other."

"But you'll find her?"

"I promise to try my best," Theodora replied, but Zada looked at Zora—or perhaps Zora looked at Zada—and they both frowned. Nobody wants to hear that you will try your best. It is the wrong thing to say. It is like saying "I probably won't hit you with a shovel." Suddenly everyone is afraid you will do the opposite.

"You must be worried sick" is what I said instead. "We would like to know all of the details of this case, so we can help you as quickly as possible."

"Come in," Zada or Zora said, and ushered us inside a room that at first seemed hopelessly tiny and quite dark. When my eyes adjusted to the dark, I could see that what had first appeared to be walls were large cardboard boxes stacked up in every available place, making the room seem smaller than it really was. The dark was real, though. It almost always is. The smell was stronger once the door was shut—so strong that my eyes watered.

"Excuse the mess," said one of the aproned women. "The Knights were just packing up to move when this dreadful thing happened. Mr. and Mrs. Knight are beside themselves with worry."

Zada's and Zora's eyes were watering too, or perhaps they were crying, but they led us through the gap between the boxes and down a dark hallway to a sitting room that appeared to have been entirely packed up and then unpacked for the occasion. A tall lamp sat in its box with its cord snaking out of it to the plug. A sofa sat half out of a box shaped like a sofa, and in two more open boxes sat two chairs holding the only things in the room that weren't ready to be carried into a truck: Mr. and Mrs. Knight. Mr. Knight's chair was bright white and his clothes dark black, and for Mrs. Knight it was the other way. They were sitting beside each other, but they did not appear to be beside themselves with worry. They looked very tired and very confused, as if we had woken them up from a dream.

"Good evening," said Mrs. Knight.

"It's morning, madam," said either Zada or Zora.

"It *does* feel cold," Mr. Knight said, as if agreeing with what someone had said, and he looked down at his own hands.

"This is S. Theodora Markson," continued one of the aproned women, "and her apprentice. They're here about your daughter's disappearance."

"Your daughter's disappearance," Mrs. Knight repeated calmly.

Her husband turned to her. "Doretta," he said, "Miss Knight has disappeared?"

"Are you sure, Ignatius dear? I don't think Miss Knight would disappear without leaving a note."

Mr. Knight continued to stare at his hands, and then blinked and looked up at us. "Oh!" he said. "I didn't realize we had visitors."

"Good evening," said Mrs. Knight.

"It's morning, madam," said either Zada or Zora, and I was afraid the whole strange conversation was about to start up all over again.

"We've come about Miss Knight," I said quickly. "We understand she's gone missing, and we'd like to help."

But Mr. Knight was looking at his hands again, and Mrs. Knight's eyes had wandered off too, toward a doorway at the back of the room, where a round little man was gazing at all of us through round little glasses. He had a small beard on his chin that looked like it was trying to escape from his nasty smile. He looked like the sort of person who would tell you that he did not have an umbrella to lend you when he actually had several and simply wanted to see you get soaked.

"Mr. and Mrs. Knight are in no state for visitors," he said. "Zada or Zora, please take them away so I can attend to my patients."

"Yes, Dr. Flammarion," one of the aproned women said with a little bow, and motioned us out of the room. I looked back and saw Dr. Flammarion drawing a long needle out of his pocket, the kind of needle doctors like to stick you with. I recognized the smell and hurried to follow the others out of the room. We made our way through a skinny hallway made skinnier by rows of boxes, and then suddenly we were in a kitchen that made me feel much better. It was not dark. The sunlight streamed in through some big, clean windows. It smelled of cinnamon, a much better scent than what I had been smelling, and either Zada or Zora hurried to the oven and pulled out a tray of cinnamon rolls that made me ache for a proper breakfast. One of the aproned women put one on a plate for me while it was still steaming. Anyone who gives you a cinnamon roll fresh from the oven is a friend for life.

"What's wrong with the Knights?" I asked after I had thanked them. "Why are they acting so strangely?"

"They must be in shock from their daughter's disappearance," Theodora said. "People sometimes act very strangely when something terrible has happened."

One of the aproned women handed Theodora a cinnamon roll and shook her head. "They've been like this for quite some time," she said. "Dr. Flammarion has been serving as their private apothecary for a few weeks now."

"What does that mean?" I asked.

"Flammarion is a tall pink bird," Theodora said.

"An apothecary," continued the woman, more helpfully, "is something like a doctor and something like a pharmacist. For years Dr. Flammarion worked at the Colophon Clinic, just outside town, before coming here to treat the Knights. He's been using a special medicine, but they just keep getting worse."

"That must have been very upsetting for Miss Knight," I said.

Zada and Zora looked very sad. "It made Miss Knight very lonely," one of them said. "It is a lonely feeling when someone you care about becomes a stranger."

"So Miss Knight has no one caring for her," Theodora said thoughtfully. The cinnamon rolls were the sort that is all curled up like a snail in its shell, and my chaperone had unraveled the roll before starting to eat it, so both of her hands were covered in icing and cinnamon. It was the wrong way to do it. She was also wrong about no one caring for Miss Knight. Zada and Zora were the ones who were beside themselves with worry. I leaned forward and looked first at Zada and then at Zora, or perhaps the other way around. And then, while my chaperone licked her fingers, I asked the question that is printed on the cover of this book.

It was the wrong question, both when I asked it and later, when I asked the question to a man wrapped in bandages. The right question in this case was "Why was she wearing an article of clothing she did not own?" but this is not an account of times when I asked the right questions, much as I wish it were.

"Miss Knight was with us yesterday morning," one of the women said, using her apron to dab at her eyes. "She was sitting right where you are sitting now, having her usual breakfast of Schoenberg Cereal. Then she spent some time in her room before going out to meet a friend."

"Who was this friend?" I asked.

"She didn't say. She just drove off, and she hasn't come back."

"She's old enough to drive?"

"Yes, she got her license a few months ago, and her parents bought her a shiny new Dilemma."

"That's a nice automobile," I said. The Dilemma was one of the fanciest automobiles manufactured. It was claimed that you could drive a Dilemma through the wall of a building and emerge without a dent or scratch, although the building might collapse.

"Mr. and Mrs. Knight give their daughter whatever she wants," the aproned woman said. "New clothes, a new car, and all sorts of equipment for her experiments."

"Experiments?"

"Miss Knight is a brilliant chemist," Zada or Zora said proudly. "She often stays up all night working on experiments in her bedroom."

"I imagine she learned that from watching you cook," I said. "This cinnamon roll is the best I have ever tasted."

Complimenting someone in an exaggerated way is known as flattery, and flattery will generally get you anything you want, but Zada and Zora were too worried to offer me a second pastry. "She probably inherited her abilities from her grandmother," the woman said. "Ingrid Nummet Knight founded Ink Inc.

when she was a young scientist, after years of experimenting with many different inks from many different creatures. Before long Ink Inc. made the Knights the wealthiest family in town. But those days are over. Ink Inc. is almost finished, and so is the town. That's why we're leaving Stain'd-by-the-Sea."

"When are you leaving?" I asked.

"Whenever the Knights give the word."

"Even if Miss Knight doesn't come back?"

"What can we do?" asked the other woman sadly. "We're only the servants."

"Then make me some tea," said an eager voice from the doorway. The bright kitchen seemed to grow darker as Dr. Flammarion strolled into the room, took a cinnamon roll without asking, and sat down loudly.

"We were talking about Miss Knight," one woman said quietly.

"Very worrisome," the apothecary agreed, with his mouth full. "But at least her parents are resting comfortably. They were shocked to hear of the disappearance. I gave them an extra injection of medicine so that they might pass the afternoon in a comfortable state of unhurried delirium."

"What medicine is it, Doctor?" I asked.

Dr. Flammarion frowned at me. "You're a curious young man," he said.

"I'm sorry, Dr. Flammarion," Theodora said. She had finished her cinnamon roll and was wiping her fingers on the photograph of the missing girl. "My apprentice has forgotten his manners."

"It's quite all right," Dr. Flammarion said. "Curiosity tends to get little boys into trouble, but he'll learn that soon enough for himself." He offered me his nasty smile like a bad gift, and then said quickly, "The medicine I gave them is called Beekabackabooka."

I have never been to medical school and am never quite sure how to spell the word "aspirin," but I still knew that Beekabackabooka is not a medicine of any kind. It didn't matter. Even without his revealing himself to be a liar, I knew there was something suspicious about Dr. Flammarion, and even without his telling me, I knew the medicine he was giving the Knights was laudanum. I recognized the smell from an incident some weeks earlier, when people had tried to sneak some into my tea. This incident is described in my account of the first wrong question, on the rare chance you have access to, or interest in, such a report.

"It must be difficult to care for Mr. and Mrs. Knight all by yourself," I said, and looked him in the eye. He blinked behind his glasses, and his beard tried harder to flee from his nasty smile.

"I'm not quite all by myself, young man," he told me. "I have a nurse who is good with a knife."

Theodora stood up. "I want to conduct a

31

thorough search of the scene of the crime," she said.

"What crime?" Dr. Flammarion said.

"What scene?" I asked.

"It seems likely a terrible crime has been committed," Theodora said firmly, with no thought to how much that would upset the two women who cared for Miss Knight.

"As the Knight family's private apothecary, I must say that I'm not sure a crime has been committed at all. Miss Knight likely just ran away, as young girls often do."

The two servants looked at each other in frustration. "She wouldn't have run away," one of them said, "not without leaving a note."

"Who knows what a wealthy young girl will do?" Dr. Flammarion said with a smooth shrug. "In any case, I told Zada it was not worth alarming the police."

"Zora," she corrected him sharply.

"I'm sorry, Zora," Dr. Flammarion said with a little bow that indicated he was not sorry at all.

"I'm Zada," she corrected him again, "but it's true. Dr. Flammarion stopped Zora from calling the police and suggested we call you instead."

"The good doctor made a good choice," Theodora said in a tone of voice she probably thought was reassuring, and then stood up and made a dramatic gesture. "Nevertheless, I would like to search the place Miss Knight was last seen. Take me to her bedroom!"

There was no arguing with S. Theodora Markson when she began to gesture dramatically, so I followed my chaperone as she followed Zada and Zora through the packed-up house, with Dr. Flammarion close behind me, his breath as unpleasant as the rest of him. Soon we were in a room I recognized from the photograph, which Theodora put down on a brand-new desk in order to rifle through the clothing in the closet. There was no sense in it. This was not the place Miss Knight was last seen. It was simply the place Zada and Zora had seen her last. The girl had driven off in a fancy automobile. It was likely someone else had seen her afterward.

"This room isn't packed up," I said.

"Miss Knight wants to do it herself," one of the women said, "but she hasn't packed up anything but a few items of clothing."

That made me ask a question that was closer to the right question than I knew. "What was she wearing when she left?"

Zada or Zora pointed to the photograph. "See for yourself," she said. "We took that photograph yesterday morning, at her request. It was a lucky thing. Now that photograph is all over town."

I looked at the picture again. Nothing seemed

familiar, but the pink hat looked out of place. "That's an unusual cap," I said. "Do you know where she got it?"

"*Snicket*," Theodora said sternly. "A young man should not take an interest in fashion. We have a crime to solve."

Dr. Flammarion smiled at me again, and I looked down at the desk rather than look at either my chaperone or this suspicious doctor. In the middle of the tidy desk was a plain white sheet of paper with nothing on it. No, Snicket, I thought. That's not right. Here and there were tiny indentations, as if something had scratched at it. I leaned down to the desk and inhaled, and for the second time since I entered the tall pen-shaped tower, I smelled a familiar scent, or really two familiar scents mixed together. The first was the scent of the sea, a strong and briny smell that still came from the seaweed of the Clusterous Forest when the wind was blowing in the direction of Stain'd-by-the-Sea.

The second scent took me a moment to identify. It smelled in a certain way that was on the tip of my tongue until I breathed it in one more time.

"Lemony," I said, but I was not saying my name out loud. I took the piece of paper over to the bed stand, turned on the reading light, and waited a minute or two for the lightbulb to get good and hot. While I waited I looked around the room, and it occurred to me that Zada and Zora were wrong. The Knight girl had started packing. She often stayed up all night in her bedroom working on scientific experiments, but there was not one piece of scientific equipment to be seen. At last the bulb was warm enough.

There are three things to know about invisible ink. The first is that most recipes for it involve lemon juice. The second is that the invisible ink becomes visible when the paper is exposed to something hot, such as a candle or a lightbulb that has been on for a few minutes. I held the paper up, very close to the lightbulb, and watched. Zada and Zora saw what I was doing and walked over to get a look. Dr. Flammarion also stepped closer. Only Theodora did not watch the paper as it warmed up, and instead took a blouse from the closet and held it up to her own body to look at herself in the mirror.

No matter how many slow and complicated mysteries I encounter in my life, I still hope that one day a slow and complicated mystery will be solved quickly and simply. An associate of mine calls this feeling "the triumph of hope over experience," which simply means that it's never going to happen, and that is what happened then. The third thing to know about invisible ink is that it hardly ever works. After several minutes of exposing the paper to heat, I looked at it and read what it had to say:

"WHEN DID YOU SEE HER LAST?"

In other words, nothing. But the curious thing was that the nothingness was finally a clue I could use.

CHAPTER THREE

"This is a fortunate day," Theodora said to me. With one gloved hand she was steering the green roadster back toward the Lost Arms, and with her other glove she was tapping me firmly on the knee. Nobody likes to be tapped on the knee. Practically nobody likes to be tapped anywhere. She kept doing it. "'Fortunate' is a word which here means fortuitous, and it's particularly fortuitous for you. It's auspicious. It's opportune. It's kismet. It's as lucky as can be. Lucky you,

Snicket! With this new case, I will reveal my routine and my methods for skip tracing."

Outside it looked like it might rain again. Inside I had the photograph of the girl in my lap. The promising young chemist looked even more annoyed, perhaps because Theodora had left sugary fingerprints all over the picture. "What shall we do first?" I asked.

"Don't talk, Snicket," Theodora said. "Fools talk while wise people listen, so listen up and I'll tell you how we will solve this case sensibly and properly. We will do six things, and for each thing, I will hold up a finger of my hand, so at the end I will be holding up six fingers and you will not be confused."

I stopped listening, of course. Theodora's sensible and proper methods of solving our previous case had led to our dangling unnecessarily from a hawser, which is a cable suspended up in the air, not a sensible or proper thing to do. I nodded solemnly at thing number one, and when she lifted a second gloved finger, I stared out the window and thought. It was surprising to me that so much of the mystery had been solved already. Dr. Flammarion was giving Ignatius and Doretta Knight heavy doses of laudanum with his hypodermic needle, leaving them mumbling and half conscious. It was not difficult to think of reasons why an apothecary would want to control the wealthiest family in town, even if they were not as wealthy as they once had been and the town was fading away to nothing. But Dr. Flammarion would have a more difficult time with a promising young chemist, who would know all about laudanum and its sleepy, dangerous ways. And so she had vanished.

The part of the story that confused me was the note. Zada and Zora had insisted that Miss Knight would have left a note if she had run away, but Dr. Flammarion had said there was no note. But I had found a sort of half note—a message written in invisible ink that hadn't worked. Miss Knight was a chemist. She would know that invisible ink hardly ever works. She also seemed to like brand-new clothes but was wearing an old hat in the picture. There's a connection, my brain said to me, between the hat and the disappearance, but I told my brain that if there was a connection, it had to think of it itself, because my eyes had spotted a bigger clue on the street outside.

"Stop the car," I said.

"Be sensible," Theodora said. "I haven't even gotten to thing number four."

"*Stop the car, please.*"

She stopped the car, perhaps because I had said "please." I stepped out onto the curb of a quiet street, although practically all of the streets in Stain'd-by-the-Sea were quiet. They were so quiet that if you drove through them on a regular basis, you would notice anything new, such as the flyers of Miss Knight printed with the word

MISSING. You would also notice an enormous automobile, particularly if it was one of the fanciest automobiles manufactured.

I was standing in front of a Dilemma. There are people in the world who care about automobiles, and there are people who couldn't care less, and then there are the people who are impressed by the Dilemma, and those people are everyone. The Dilemma is such a tremendous thing to look at that I stared at it for a good ten seconds before reminding myself that I should think of it as a clue to a mystery rather than as a wonder of modern engineering. It was one of the newer models, with a small, old-fashioned horn perched just outside each front window, and a shiny crank on the side so you could roll down the roof if Stain'd-by-the-Sea ever offered pleasant weather, and it was the color of someone buying you an ice cream cone for no reason at all.

Theodora had gotten out of the roadster and

stared at the Dilemma for as long as I had. "You should be ashamed of yourself, Snicket," she said, when she had remembered to be a chaperone. "You're supposed to be looking for Miss Knight, not getting distracted by automobiles, no matter how beautiful they are and how interesting to behold and no matter how long you want to stand here staring at it because it's very beautiful and interesting to behold and so you find yourself staring at it for quite some time because it is so beautiful and interesting—"

"This car probably belongs to Miss Knight," I said before she could continue. "Not many people can afford a new Dilemma."

"Then she must be nearby," Theodora said, turning quickly all the way around to look in every direction down the empty street.

"I read once," I said, "about a person who parked their car and then went someplace else."

"Don't be impertinent." Theodora frowned. "Where could she have gone?"

I looked down the block. "Impertinent" is a word which actually means "not suitable to the circumstances," but most people use it to mean "I am using a complicated word in the hopes that it will make you stop talking," so I merely pointed at the only remaining grocery store in town.

Partial Foods must have once been a grand grocery store. It was not a grand grocery store for the duration of my stay in Stain'd-by-the-Sea. It looked like a grand grocery store that someone had thrown down the stairs. To enter the store, you walked through a pair of enormous glass doors with brass handles carved with images of fresh fruit and vegetables, but the doors were badly cracked and difficult to open. There were wide shelves and deep bins ready to hold enormous mountains of delicious food, but at least half of them were empty, and the rest held food that was unripe or stale, mushy or brittle, bruised or encased in too many layers of plastic, or something I didn't like. The place was almost enormous and almost deserted, so it took some time wandering through the big, meager aisles until we found someone to talk to. The owner of Partial Foods was a woman who could look both very angry and very bored at the same time and in fact was doing so when we found her. On a stained smock, she was wearing a peeled name tag that read POLLY PARTIAL.

"Good day," Theodora said to her.

"Who are you?" Polly Partial asked. She was standing next to a basket of honeydew melons. I do not like honeydew melons. I do not see the point of them.

"My name is S. Theodora Markson, and this is my apprentice," Theodora said, and took the flyer from my hand. "We're looking for this person."

Polly Partial peered at the frowning girl. "That's Cleo Knight," she said, pointing to the words printed above the photograph.

"Yes, we know," Theodora said. "I was wondering if you had seen her recently."

"Hard to say," Polly Partial said. "She looks like any other runaway girl, even if she is from a wealthy family. Is there a reward? With enough money, I could retire and devote myself to raising minks."

The Knights had not said anything about a reward, but Theodora did not say anything about there not being one. "Only if you help us," she said. "Have you seen this girl?"

The shopkeeper squinted at the flyer. "Yesterday morning," she said, "about ten thirty. She hurried in here to buy that silly breakfast food she likes." She led us down an aisle and pulled down a box for us to see. It was Schoenberg Cereal, the brand Zada and Zora had mentioned. TWELVE WHOLESOME GRAINS COMBINED IN A STRICT SEQUENCE, the label read. I could not imagine who would eat such a thing in a kitchen where fresh-baked cinnamon rolls could be had.

"The Knights are the only ones who buy it," Polly Partial said, "although usually it's one of those twin servants who does the shopping."

"Did she say anything?" Theodora asked.

"She said thanks," Polly said, "and then she said she was running away to join the circus."

My chaperone scratched her hair. "The circus?"

"That's what she said," said Polly Partial.

"*Aha!*" Theodora cried.

"Then she walked outside and got into a taxicab and went off."

"*Aha!*"

I didn't see anything to *aha!* about, but I've never been an *aha!* sort of person. "What was she wearing?" I asked.

Theodora gave me an exasperated sigh. "What did I tell you about your interest in fashion?" she said. "A young man who asks too much about clothing will find himself the subject of unflattering rumors."

"You can see for yourself what she was wearing," Polly Partial said, and handed me back the flyer. "The Knight family always wears black and white, to honor the family business and the paper it's scrawled on. I remember the hat surprised me. It wasn't black and it wasn't white. It looked French."

"You've been very helpful, Ms. Partial," Theodora said. "I'm sure the Knights will thank you."

"Of course, everything looks French when you stop to think about it."

"You're a very reliable witness," I couldn't help saying, and Polly Partial looked at me like she had never seen me before.

"Off with you," she said. "I have canned smelt to stack."

We left the store and stood in the street. Overhead the clouds talked with the wind about whether or not it should rain again. "Well, I'd say the case is solved," Theodora said, and her hair ruffled in agreement. "Dr. Flammarion was right. There is no crime. The Knight girl ran away from home. She drove into town, bought the supplies she needed, and took a taxi to join the circus. Do you have any questions?"

I had so many questions that they fought for a minute in my head over which one got to ask itself first. "Why didn't she need more than cereal?" was the winner. "Why didn't she leave a note?" was in second place, followed by "Why wouldn't she run away in her car?"

Theodora waved her gloved hand at me like I was a bad smell. "Be sensible," she said. "There is no indication of a crime. I'm going to write the report myself so I get full credit for solving the case."

"We should investigate further," I said.

"That's what you said last time," Theodora reminded me, putting on her helmet and opening the door of the roadster, "and the only thing you investigated was that silly girl. Girls and fashion, Snicket. You are too easily distracted."

I felt myself blush. It is not a feeling I like. My ears get hot, and my face gets red, and it is no way to win an argument. "I'm going to walk back to the Lost Arms if you don't mind," I said. "It's only a couple of blocks."

"By all means," Theodora said. "You'd only be a fifth wheel if you hung around our head-quarters while I wrote my report. In fact, Snicket, why don't you make yourself scarce until dinner-time?"

She shut the door of the roadster and drove off. I waited for the sound of the engine to fade, and then spent another minute looking once more at the Dilemma. I even put out a hand and rested my palm on one of the horns. "A fifth wheel" is an expression meaning some-one who is of no help at all, the way a fifth wheel on an automobile doesn't make it go any faster.

It made no sense that Miss Knight would drive to Partial Foods and then take a taxi someplace else. She would never need a taxi at all, with an automobile like that. But she did. But she wouldn't. But she did. Stop arguing with yourself, Snicket. You can't win. I looked down at the ground and wished I'd looked there earlier. One of the tires of the Dilemma was deflated, so instead of looking round, it looked like an old potato. You couldn't drive far like that. A Dilemma with a flat tire was a reminder that no matter how splendid and shiny the world might be, it could be spoiled by something you didn't notice until the damage had been done.

I leaned down to get a closer look and found myself staring at a needle. It was the kind of needle doctors like to stick you with, and it was sticking out of the flattened tire.

"Hello," I said to the needle.

The needle didn't say anything, and neither

did anybody else. I slipped the needle out of the tire. It didn't smell like anything, but you wouldn't have to inject a tire with laudanum. Flattening it would be enough. Carefully, so I wouldn't get punctured, I put the needle in my pocket and stood up and looked this way and that. No one was around. Like most blocks in town, this block was nothing but boarded-up shops and homes and flyers with Cleo Knight staring back at me. But there was also someplace I'd been meaning to visit since my arrival in town. Why not now? I thought.

Hungry's was a small and narrow place, and a large and wide woman was standing just inside the doors, polishing the counter with a rag. "Good afternoon," she said.

I said the same thing.

"I'm hungry," she said.

"Well, you're probably in the right place."

She gave me a frown and a menu. "No, I mean

I'm Hungry. It's my name. Hungry Hix. I own this place. Are you hungry?"

"No," I said. "You are."

"Don't be a smart aleck," Hungry said.

"But it cheers me up," I said.

"Sit anywhere you want," she said. "A waiter will be right with you."

There were a few booths alongside one wall, but I always like sitting at the counter. There was a boy a few years older than I was, leaning against a sink full of dirty dishes with a book in his hand and shaggy red hair in his eyes. I had not heard of the book, but I liked the author.

"How's that book?"

"Good," he said, without looking up. "A guy named Johnny takes the wrong train and ends up in Constantinople in 1453. This guy's books are always good."

"That's true," I said, "but there's a bunch of books that he didn't really write. They put his name on them anyway. You have to check carefully to make sure you don't get one of those."

"Is that so?" he said, and put down the book and poured me a glass of water and shook my hand. "I'm Jake Hix," he said. "I haven't seen you in here before."

"I'm Lemony Snicket and I've never been in here," I said. "Are you Hungry's son?"

"Hungry's my aunt," Jake said. "I work for her in exchange for room and board."

"I know the feeling," I said. "I'm an apprentice myself."

"An apprentice what?"

"It's a long story," I said.

"I have time."

"No you don't," Hungry grumbled, squeezing by Jake and swatting him with a towel. "Take his order and do the dishes."

"Never mind her," Jake said, when his aunt was out of earshot. "She's cranky because business is bad. Few people come in here anymore. This town is draining like somebody pulled the plug. You're the first paying customer we've had all day."

"I don't have any money," I said.

Jake shrugged. "If you're hungry, I'll make you something," he said. "It's better than doing dishes. You like soup?"

Never say you're hungry until you learn what they're fixing. "I like good soup," I said.

"Good soup it is," Jake said with a smile. "With dumplings."

Jake busied himself at the stove, and I put the flyer down on the counter. "Have you seen this person?" I asked.

Jake looked quickly at the photograph and then looked away. "Of course," he said. "That's the Knight girl. Those flyers are all over town."

"I'm looking for her," I said.

"Everybody is, it looks like."

"You said few people come in here," I told him. "Was she one of them?"

Jake turned away from me and chopped

something very hard and very quickly before throwing it into a pan to sizzle. "I don't talk about my customers," he said.

"If she's in trouble," I said, "I can help."

Jake turned around then and gave me a look like I was a fifth wheel after all. It didn't look like he really meant it, but I still didn't like getting it. "You?" he asked. "Some stranger who just wandered into the diner?"

"I'm not a stranger," I said, and pointed to his book. "I read the same authors you do."

Jake thought about this for a minute, and the food started to smell good. "Miss Knight was in here yesterday morning," he said, "about ten thirty."

"Ten thirty?" I asked. "Are you sure about that?"

"Sure I'm sure," he said.

"Did she have breakfast?"

"Tea," he said. "It helps her think."

"Did she say anything?"

Jake gave me a curious look. "She said thanks."

"Anything else?"

"I don't know what you've heard, Snicket, but Miss Knight's not a friend of mine. She's just a customer."

"What was she wearing?"

"The same as in the picture."

"Let me guess," I said. "Then she got into a taxi."

"A taxi?" Jake repeated with a laugh. "You really are a stranger. Cleo in a taxi! Miss Knight's got a brand-new Dilemma that's way better than any taxi."

"There's no need to insult us, Jake," said a voice from the door.

Two boys had walked into Hungry's, and they were two boys I knew. Their names were Bouvard Bellerophon and Pecuchet Bellerophon, which explains why everyone called them Pip and Squeak. They worked as taxi drivers when their father was sick, and it looked like he was sick today. I said hello and they said hello and Jake said hello and we figured out we all knew one another.

"I'm making Snicket here some soup," Jake said. "You two want some?"

"Absolutely," Pip said. "Business is slow today."

"Then can you give me a ride after lunch?" I asked them.

"Sure," said Squeak in the voice that matched his nickname. "We're parked right outside. Going to see your friend again, in Handkerchief Heights?"

"She doesn't live there anymore," I said, not wanting to say Ellington's name, "and I don't know if I'd call her a friend, exactly."

"That's too bad," Pip said. "She seemed nice enough to me."

"I'd rather not talk about it," I said. "How's your father?"

"We'd rather not talk about that," Squeak said.

"Well, then what should we talk about?"

"Books," Jake said, and served up soup. After one bite I knew where I'd be eating for the duration. The dumplings had the flavor of paradise, and the broth spread through my veins like a secret that's fun to keep. I wanted to tell the secret to my sister, who would have enjoyed the soup, but she was back in the city, doing the wrong things while I was asking the wrong questions, so I couldn't share it with her. Pip and Squeak probably wanted to share the soup with their father, and I had a feeling as to whom Jake would like to share it with. But we didn't talk about that. We talked about the author of the book he was reading. It felt good. I finished my soup and wiped my mouth and asked if there was anything else he could think of to tell me about Miss Cleo Knight. He said there wasn't. He wasn't telling me the truth, but I couldn't get sore about it. I wasn't telling everyone my business either. I stood up, and Pip and Squeak stood up, and we walked out of Hungry's to the cab. Squeak got in and hunched down by the brake and gas pedals, and Pip arranged some books so he could sit on them and reach the steering wheel. I got in back, moving carefully so I wouldn't get punctured by the needle in my pocket.

"Where are we going, Snicket?" Pip asked me.

"To the lighthouse," I said, which reminded me of a book I'd been meaning to read. "I need a haircut."

CHAPTER FOUR

The lighthouse at the edge of Stain'd-by-the-Sea probably seemed like a fifth wheel to most people who saw it. Once it had towered over a cliff overlooking the churning waters of the sea, but since the sea had been drained away there were only a few remaining inkwells and the great, spooky expanse of the Clusterous Forest under the lighthouse's watch. No ships could sail there, so there was no need for them to be guided by a beam of light. Furthermore, the lighthouse had once been the headquarters for Stain'd-by-the-Sea's only newspaper, *The Stain'd Lighthouse*, but nowadays there was not enough ink for the news and hardly any people to read it.

But the lighthouse was not a fifth wheel, as there was someone who lived there who was still a fine journalist, even though *The Stain'd Lighthouse* had shut down. Her name was Moxie Mallahan, and she was a friend of mine, although she didn't look very friendly as she opened the door.

"What's the news, Moxie?" I said.

She frowned at me in her usual brimmed hat which, today at least, also seemed to be frowning. "Lemony Snicket," she said.

It's rarely good when someone says your full name, except perhaps when it's at the end of "I have a package for." "I know I haven't been around lately, Moxie," I said.

"I was bored," Moxie said. "You know there

66

aren't many people our age left in this town."

"Don't get sore," I said. "I've found us something I'm sure you'll find interesting."

"If it's something to do with that girl who took that statue," Moxie said, "I'm not interested at all."

Moxie had helped me out on my previous case and had seen Ellington Feint disappear with the Bombinating Beast. "This has nothing to do with her," I said, without saying her name and without knowing I was wrong.

Moxie didn't stop frowning, but she looked like she was thinking of stopping. "So?"

"I'm looking for the Knight girl."

"You and everybody else in town," Moxie said. "I've seen that poster up everywhere."

"Theodora and I are on the case," I said, "but I need your help."

She looked at me and thought. Behind her I could see the typewriter, which folded up into its own case. Moxie always had her typewriter handy so that she might take notes on what was going on. I knew her curiosity about things that went on in town meant she would let me into her home, and I was right. Before I stepped inside, I called to the Bellerophon brothers and asked them if they'd mind waiting. They didn't, as long as I'd give them another tip if they gave me another ride. I said sure. The tip I'd given them for the ride to the lighthouse was the tip about the author's books that aren't really written by the author. It was an old tip, as I had already given it to Jake Hix. But it was the only tip I had handy.

I followed Moxie into her kitchen. There was a pot of coffee bubbling away, so I knew her father was somewhere close by, but Moxie did not mention him, just sat me down at the table and put her typewriter between us.

"What's going on with the case?" she asked. "Where is Cleo Knight? When did she go missing? Who have you talked to? How about some tea?"

"No, thank you," I said, answering only the last question. "But I was hoping you could cut my hair. I haven't seen a barbershop in town."

"The last one closed," she said, "but I'm not cutting your hair, Snicket, until you tell me what's going on."

"I'll tell you," I said, "while you cut my hair. A haircut can help solve this case. Get a bowl, will you?"

She gave me a skeptical look. Being skeptical is a good thing for a journalist, because it means you don't completely trust anyone. I tried to give her an it's-good-to-be-skeptical-but-please-don't-be-skeptical-right-now look back. I don't know if my look was understood, but she fetched a pair of scissors and a small bowl, which she placed upside down on my head. It is my great hope that this portion of the story, should it ever be published, is not illustrated, as a person looks like a fool with a bowl over his head. Moxie clicked the blades of the scissors together and started cutting, and I started my story.

"Cleo Knight woke up yesterday morning and had her usual breakfast of Schoenberg Cereal," I said. "She was wearing brand-new clothes that were black and white, and an old hat that was somewhat pink. She ran away to join the circus and didn't leave a note, but that couldn't have happened, because she's a brilliant chemist, not a circus performer, and the people who know her best say she definitely would have left a note. She was seen at Partial Foods by Polly Partial at ten thirty buying Schoenberg Cereal and leaving in a taxicab, but that couldn't have happened, because she'd driven there in her brand-new Dilemma."

"That's a nice car," Moxie said.

"Mind the ears," I said. "Now, Cleo Knight was also seen at Hungry's by Jake Hix, also at ten thirty, and she left in the Dilemma. But

that can't have happened, because the Dilemma is parked nearby with a flat tire."

"That's a lot of things that couldn't have happened," Moxie said.

"Either Polly Partial is wrong," I said, "or Jake Hix is wrong."

"Or they're both wrong."

"That's true. Do you know either of them?"

"I know both of them," Moxie said, "but not that well. It's the Knights I'm thinking about, though. They must be worried sick."

"The housekeepers are worried sick," I said. "Mr. and Mrs. Knight are in a state of unhurried delirium."

"I don't know what that means," Moxie said, moving around to the back of my head.

"It means their personal apothecary is giving them regular injections of laudanum," I said. "It's a drug that makes you sleepy and strange. What do you know about the Knight family?"

Moxie walked around to face me and frowned.

I could not tell if she was frowning at the thought of the Knights or at the way she'd cut my hair. "Well, Ingrid Nummet Knight, Cleo's grandmother, was the genius who founded Ink Inc. along with her business partner, Colonel Colophon, our town's greatest war hero. Ingrid died some time ago and left the company to her son, Ignatius Nettle Knight. Cleo's father is not a genius at all, nor a scientist. He is a tycoon, which is a sort of businessperson, and business has not gone well."

"You can say that again."

"Business has not gone well."

"Cut it out, Moxie. What happened to the business partner?"

"Colonel Colophon has suffered terrible injuries."

"War is terrible," I said.

"Yes it is," Moxie said, "but Colonel Colophon was not injured in the war. He was injured at the unveiling of the statue in his honor. It was a huge statue, right in front of the library, depicting him untangling a child's kite from a tree while a battle raged all around him. But there was an explosion at the unveiling, and the colonel suffered terrible burns. There was a special clinic built, way out on the outskirts of town, to help him with his injuries. The colonel was wrapped up in so many bandages he looked like a mummy. He's lived at the clinic ever since. I'm too young to remember, but I'm sure there was a picture in the paper. I can find it for you if you like."

"No, thank you," I said. "I know what a mummy looks like. But back to the Knight family, please. How did Cleo's father ruin the business?"

"It was his idea to drain the sea so that Ink Inc. might harvest the last of the octopi inkwells. It turned out to be a very expensive plan."

"Expensive or not, if he hadn't done that, there'd be no ink in this town at all."

"That's what's going to happen anyway,"

Moxie said sadly, and put down her scissors. "The last of the octopi live down in those wells. One day those enormous needles will find that they've poked the very last one, and then nothing will be left. I don't like to think about it."

"I don't like needles either," I said, and took one out of my pocket.

"What's that?" Moxie asked.

"A different sort of needle," I said. "The kind a doctor might use."

"You shouldn't carry a hypodermic needle around in your pocket, Snicket."

"That's true," I said. "It could puncture me. This needle's big enough to puncture a tire."

"Such as the tire of the Dilemma," Moxie said. "Is that where you found it?"

"You're a very good journalist, Moxie."

"Yes," Moxie said, "but I'm not a very good barber."

She took the bowl off my head and held up a frying pan, shiny enough so that I might look at my reflection. It was nothing I would want to see illustrated, but it was not so very ghastly.

"You look like Stew Mitchum," she said.

"Thank you."

"That's not what I meant. What I mean is, how are you going to use that haircut to stop that doctor?"

"Stop Dr. Flammarion?"

"Don't you suspect him?"

"Well, he's suspicious," I said, "but why would he kidnap Cleo?"

"To get ransom money from the Knights."

"They're in such a state of unhurried delirium that he could steal whatever he wanted without going to the trouble of kidnapping. Besides, most of the ink money is gone."

Moxie sighed and gave me a careful look. "Is this Hangfire's work?"

"Well," I said, "it's wickedness. But exactly what kind of wickedness is what I'm going to find out."

"You and Theodora?" she asked me.

"Theodora believes the circus story."

"What do you believe?"

"I believe I need to go back into town," I said.

"I believe I need to go with you."

"Moxie—"

"Don't argue with me, Snicket. I want to find out what's going on. Now sweep up your hair while I take some notes."

I found a broom, and Moxie turned to her typewriter. I swept and she typed furiously. Some people are so sentimental that they keep locks of hair from people they love, but nobody wanted what I was sweeping. I thought of Ellington Feint's missing father and wondered if he'd left anything behind that she kept, for sentimental reasons. Moxie typed even faster, as if she knew what I was thinking about and it annoyed her. I dumped my hair into the trash, and she closed her typewriter.

"Let's go," Moxie said.

"Don't you have to tell your father you're going out?"

"I'm going out!" she called to her father, and we walked out of the lighthouse and up to the waiting taxi.

"Back into town, Snicket?" Pip asked, as his brother crawled down to the pedals.

"Partial Foods, please," I said, "and if you like stories about strange happenings, allow me to recommend a book about a girl named Amanda, who is either a witch or a stepsister or both."

Pip started up the motor and handed me a scrap of paper. "Sounds good," he said. "Write down the title for me, will you?"

"He will if you answer a question," Moxie piped up. "Pip, did you and your brother take Cleo Knight anywhere yesterday morning, say about ten thirty?"

It is difficult to actually kick yourself in the back of an automobile, so I just imagined doing it, for failing to ask this question myself.

"Cleo Knight's never been in our cab," Squeak said from the floor, "and I can't say I blame her, with a Dilemma like that."

"Then Polly Partial was lying," Moxie murmured to me, "and Jake Hix was telling the truth."

I put a picture of Polly Partial in my head, and then one of Jake Hix right next to it. The grocer was an unpleasant person, but she didn't seem like a liar. Jake Hix, on the other hand, seemed like a decent fellow who read good books and cooked good soup. But even though I didn't know what the truth was, I knew he hadn't told me it when I'd asked about Cleo Knight.

"It's good to know who are the bad guys and who are the good guys," Moxie continued, but I shook my head. It is often said that people do things because they are good or evil, but in my experience that is not the case. Ellington Feint, for example, had lied to me and stolen, but not because she was an evil person. She was a good person, forced to do bad things in order to free her father from Hangfire's clutches. My sister, for another example, was certainly a good person, but she was soon to commit a crime with one of the items in the museum. As far as I could tell, people didn't do things because they were good or evil. They did things because they could not think of what else to do, and the only thing I could think of was finding out what was going on in this town.

"Here we are," Pip said, tapping his brother to put on the brakes. "Partial Foods. Want me to wait again, Snicket?"

"No, thanks," I said, and handed him the scrap of paper. "Can you read that long word? It's 'headless.'"

Pip nodded at me, but he was looking somewhere far past the windshield. Moxie and I got out of the car, and the Bellerophon brothers drove off down the empty street. "Stay close,"

I told the journalist, "but you don't want to be seen with me right now."

Moxie opened up her typewriter. "Why not?"

"Because I'm about to be arrested," I said, and strode into the supermarket. It looked as tired as usual, with a few customers here and there among the aisles of exhausted food. I paced through the place for a few minutes, and Moxie paced along with me, although always in a different aisle and always with a look on her face like she was searching for a particular item. She was good at it. I found Polly Partial soon enough, wheeling a large stack of canned soup toward a remote corner of the place.

"Hello," I said. "Nice to see you again."

Polly frowned. "I don't remember you."

"I knocked over a display once," I said, "and sent pineapples tumbling all over the place."

"Oh yes," Polly said, and blew some air into her frown so it was bigger.

"No," I said, "that wasn't me." I turned on my heel and walked quickly toward the basket of honeydew melons. Wherever you can find a honeydew melon, you can find other melons. All other melons are better. There is really no point to having a honeydew melon under any circumstances whatsoever. I picked up two honeydew melons in my hands, checked to make sure Polly Partial was watching me, and then dashed quickly out the door. I heard Moxie gasp.

"Stop, thief!" Polly Partial called to me. "Stop or I'll call the police!"

Of course I didn't stop. The police were who I wanted called.

CHAPTER FIVE

I heard the police siren sooner than I would have thought. I'd had just enough time to kneel down next to the curb and quickly hide the honeydew melons under the Dilemma. I stood up and brushed off my pants just as the dented station wagon of Stain'd-by-the-Sea's only police officers pulled up in front of Partial Foods. As usual, there was a red flashlight taped to the roof of the car, instead of a police car's usual flashing light, and the siren sound came from a boy about my age sitting in the backseat. Stew Mitchum had the ability to mimic the irritating sound of a siren, and this was not the only irritating ability he had displayed to me. He was the sort of child who was nasty to everyone but behaved like an angel when his parents were watching. There is nothing to be done about such people in the world. It is best not even to talk to them, but Stew saw me and hopped out of the automobile while his parents walked into Partial Foods. Harvey and Mimi Mitchum were arguing, as they were always doing, and Stew had his usual wicked smile.

"I thought you'd left town, Lemon Drop," he said to me. "Stain'd-by-the-Sea doesn't have room for idiots."

"Really?" I said. "I heard they could get jobs as police sirens."

"I'm glad you think police work is so funny," Stew said. "My parents got a report of a young thief at Partial Foods. You wouldn't know any-thing about that, would you?"

"I'm just here to admire this Dilemma," I said, "and of course to chat with a charming person such as yourself."

"Call me charming again and I'll slug you," Stew growled, but then he had to give me a wide, friendly smile, because the Officers Mitchum were coming back out of the supermarket.

"Mommy! Daddy!" Stew said, and ran to the officers. "I missed you so much."

"What a sweetheart," said Mimi Mitchum, as her son gave her a large, false hug. "We missed you too, Stewie. But we have a crime to solve."

"An *important* crime," corrected her husband.

"All crime is important, Harvey."

"But some crimes are more important than others."

"I don't think we should argue about it in front of the B-O-Y."

"Stewart knows how to spell 'boy,' Mimi. There's no reason to spell it out."

"And there's no reason for you to boss me around like that, Harvey."

"Mimi—"

"Don't Mimi me, Harvey."

"Well, don't Harvey me."

"How can I not Harvey you when your name's Harvey?"

I hadn't been in Stain'd-by-the-Sea very long, but I'd long ago learned the Officers Mitchum would continue arguing until someone interrupted them. "Hello, Officers," I said. "I haven't seen you for quite some time."

Harvey and Mimi Mitchum stopped scowling at each other and turned their gaze to me. They had a look on their faces that they probably thought was intimidating. "Intimidating" is a word meaning it was supposed to scare me, but instead I just wondered what they had eaten recently that made them frown.

"Lemony Snicket," Harvey Mitchum said. "The last time we saw you was during all that unpleasantness with the stolen statue, and now here you are at the scene of another theft."

"A theft?" I said. "Egad!"

"Don't talk with four-letter words," Mimi Mitchum said to me, covering Stewie's ears.

"There are four four-letter words in the sentence 'Don't talk with four-letter words,'" I said. I was being cheeky, but I was afraid that if I were polite, I might not get arrested.

"That's it," Harvey Mitchum said. "You're under arrest, Snicket. Come with us."

He grabbed my arm, and then Mimi Mitchum said that she ought to be the one to be taking my arm because he had taken the arms of the last three people they had arrested, and Harvey said it didn't matter one way or another who took the arm of someone they were arresting, and Mimi said if it didn't matter who took the arm of someone they arrested, why couldn't she be the one taking my arm, and he said he'd prefer not to talk about it any further in front of the B-O-Y, and Mimi reminded him that he had reminded her that their intelligent, sensitive boy could certainly spell a simple three-letter word, as opposed to me, who used four-letter words all the time and needed to be arrested right away. It was interesting to watch Stewie's face as his parents bickered. He reminded me of a shark I had seen once in the aquarium, circling a tank while schoolchildren tapped on the glass. Someday, the shark seemed to be thinking, I will no longer be trapped like this. I will be in the open water, right where you'll be swimming. On that day you'd better watch out.

But it was not Stew who interrupted the bickering Mitchums. "What's going on, Officers?" Moxie Mallahan said, stepping out of Partial Foods and reaching into the brim of her hat. She kept cards there, printed with her name and occupation. She handed one to each of the Mitchums to remind them who she was. They did not look happy to be reminded.

"This is police business," said the male Officer Mitchum. "There was a honeydew theft at Partial Foods, and we are just arresting a suspect."

"Who are you arresting?" Moxie asked. "Why have you arrested him? How did you decide he was a suspect? What evidence do you have? Where are the melons?"

"This young man," Mimi Mitchum said, pointing at me, "was seen loitering outside the supermarket. He has a history of suspicious activities. We're bringing him down to the police station to be identified by the witness. It's still too early to make assumptions, but it wouldn't be surprising if this Snicket lad here ends up in jail for a very long time."

The Officers Mitchum always said it was too early to make assumptions. They apparently enjoyed doing things early. "Mind if I tag along?" Moxie asked. "I'd like to see how this plays out."

"There are no newspapers left in this town," Harvey Mitchum said suspiciously. "How can you be a journalist?"

"That's the wrong question," Moxie said with a small smile. "The question is, how can a town find out what's going on if nobody's there to report it?"

The Officers Mitchum grunted and shrugged, and opened the back door of the station wagon to pile us all in. Moxie went in first and then me and then Stew. It is uncomfortable to sit in the middle seat, but Stew had a habit of pinching people, and I thought Moxie would want to avoid that. It was the least I could do. After a short argument over who should drive, Mimi started the engine and Stew made his siren noise out the window as we drove through town.

The police station at Stain'd-by-the-Sea was half of a building that had once been City Hall. The other half was the library, where I spent a great deal of my time. The building was a shadow of its former self, which means that it once looked nice but now was as fading as anything else in town, with two big, crumbling pillars and a set of front stairs covered in cracks. Harvey Mitchum took me out of the car, and Moxie and Stew followed behind us while Mimi Mitchum turned the station wagon around and drove away. We walked across the lawn to the building, passing a sculpture so damaged I could never identify it. I looked at it differently this time. I thought of a war hero, and the day the statue was unveiled.

The police station turned out to be one long room, about the size of a bus. At the back of the bus was Stain'd-by-the-Sea's only jail cell, with thick metal bars and a small cot for a prisoner to sleep on. There was no prisoner, asleep or awake. The rest of the room was taken up with desks, chairs, cabinets, tables, and endless piles of paper that make every office look the same and boring.

"Now look here, Snicket," Harvey Mitchum said to me. "We're doing this by the book. Polly Partial said a boy about your age stole two honeydew melons from her store. Mimi is bringing her here now to identify you from a lineup, which is a police term for people lined up." He stomped his way to a drawer and pulled out three dirty caps and three large squares of cardboard with loops of string stapled to them. He frowned and pointed me toward a blank and dirty wall. "Go stand over there," he barked, "and put these on."

He handed me a cap and a cardboard square. The cap advertised the Stain'd-by-the-Sea Sea Stains, a sports team that no longer existed, and the cardboard square turned out to be a sign with the number 1 scrawled on it. "Son," he said to Stew, "would you please do me a favor and stand next to the boy we just arrested?"

Stew turned around so his father couldn't see him sneering at me, and then stood next to me while his father hung a cap and a sign on him. Stew's cap was the same. His sign read *B*.

"We need a third person," Officer Mitchum muttered, and cast his eyes around the room. He stopped at Moxie, who was already typing into her typewriter. "Young lady," he said, "I need your help."

"Of course, Officer," she said.

"Please help me move that small file cabinet so it's next to those two boys," Harvey Mitchum said, and together the police officer and the journalist dragged the file cabinet until it was standing in line with Stew and me. The officer nodded at his handiwork and balanced a cap and a sign on top of the cabinet. The cabinet's sign was scrawled with a simple star, the sort a teacher writes at the top of a piece of homework to indicate that you've either done the assignment well or she hasn't read it carefully.

The three of us stood there for a minute. I don't know what Stew was thinking, and the filing cabinet wasn't thinking anything. But I was thinking, is this the world? Is this really the place in which you've ended up, Snicket? It was a question that struck me, as it might strike you, when something ridiculous was going on, or something sad. I wondered if this was really where I should be, or if there was another world someplace, less ridiculous and less sad. But I never knew the answer to the question. Perhaps I had been in another world before I was born, and did not remember it, or perhaps I would see another world when I died, which I was in no hurry to do. In the meantime I knew only the world I was in. In the meantime I was stuck in this police station, doing something so ridiculous it felt sad, and feeling so sad that it was ridiculous. The world of the police station, the world of Stain'd-by-the-Sea and all of the wrong questions I was asking, was the only world I could see.

"Close your eyes," Harvey Mitchum said. "Close your eyes until I tell you different."

I closed my eyes and heard the shuffle of two people entering the police station. "Here we are, Ms. Partial," Mimi Mitchum said. "Take a good look at this lineup we have for you."

"Is one of them the thief?"

"That's for you to tell us, ma'am. Remember, you can see everyone in the lineup, but they cannot see you. Now then, do you recognize any of these three individuals? Is the thief who robbed your store number 1, number B, or number Star?"

There was a small, busy silence as Polly Partial

looked us over. Even Moxie paused in her typing.

"Number B," she said finally. "Yes, it's number B. That's the thief!"

I heard Harvey Mitchum take a deep breath. "How dare you!" he thundered when it was done. "Number B is my boy, Stew. He couldn't have taken those honeydews. He has been with me all day long, and he never eats fresh fruit or vegetables."

"I don't like how they taste," explained Stew, next to me.

"And you don't have to, my darling," Mimi Mitchum cooed.

"Number B is the only one I recognize," the grocer insisted. "I would swear on my mother's grave, if only she were dead."

"We're very grateful for your help, Ms. Partial," Harvey Mitchum said in an ungrateful voice. "My wife will drive you back to your store."

"Why should I have to drive her?" asked the

female Officer Mitchum. "Why don't you drive for a change?"

"Because you have the keys to the car, Mimi."

"So now I have to drive *and* hold the keys to the car? Why don't you just put your feet up on the desk as usual, if I'm doing all the work of the Stain'd-by-the-Sea police force?"

"I don't put my feet up on the desk!"

"Of course you do! You take them down when I walk into the station, but you can't fool me, Harvey. I have eyes like an ostrich."

"Ostriches don't have particularly good eyes. I think you mean an eagle."

"Don't tell me what I mean!"

"Well, don't tell me you're an ostrich when you're really an eagle!"

"I'm a *woman*, Harvey. Don't call me a bird, you imbecile!"

"Don't call me an imbecile, you fool!"

"Don't call me a fool, you numbskull!"

"Never mind," Polly Partial said. "I'd rather

walk back to my supermarket. Good day, Officers."

The Officers Mitchum muttered something I could not hear over the sound of Moxie's typewriter, and then I heard Ms. Partial's footsteps heading out the door and down the stairs. "You can open your eyes now, son," Harvey Mitchum said with a sigh. "You too, Snicket."

Apparently, the file cabinet had to keep its eyes closed. I removed my hat and my sign and handed them back to the officer.

"I still think you had something to do with this crime," he said, "but I have no proof."

"Her eyesight might be bad," his wife said. "Polly Partial is no spring chicken."

"I'd call her an autumn chicken," Harvey Mitchum agreed, "or even a winter chicken. She couldn't recognize a lampshade if I put it on her head."

"It might be her eyesight," I said, "or it might be that she sees so many people come in and out of her store that she can't tell them apart. The point is that she's not a reliable witness."

"You're right," Harvey Mitchum admitted, and sat down at one of the desks. "Well, at least we solved one crime today. That's not bad."

"True," Mimi Mitchum agreed. "We did manage to close the Knight case." She took a handkerchief out of her pocket, licked one corner of it, and tried to rub some dirt off Stew's squirming face. Moxie and I shared a look.

"That missing girl?" I asked.

"Miss Knight is not missing," Harvey said, and put his feet up on the desk. "We noticed the posters around town and wondered why nobody had called us, but we ran into your associate Theodora and she told us that there was no crime. Miss Knight was seen running away to join the circus."

"The person who saw her couldn't recognize a lampshade if I put it on her head."

Mimi looked sharply at Harvey and pushed his feet off the desk before looking just as sharply at me. "What do you mean?" she demanded.

I looked over at Moxie, and the journalist tipped her hat at me and gave me a little shrug. I knew what the shrug meant. It meant that the Officers Mitchum were not good police officers but they were good people. They would try to help someone in trouble. They would fail, but at least they would try, even if the trouble was only a couple of stolen melons that nobody should eat. Cleo Knight was probably in much worse trouble, and so I should tell them what I knew, even if I thought they would be of little assistance. That was a lot to put into a shrug, but it is like that with good journalists. It is like that with good friends.

"Polly Partial saw somebody buying cereal and getting into a cab, but it wasn't Cleo Knight. Ms. Partial didn't recognize me when I got a haircut, and she couldn't tell your son from a file cabinet."

Stew was sticking his tongue out at me, but his parents were listening closely. "Then where is the Knight girl?" Mimi asked.

"There are two people who might know," I said. "One is Jake Hix, who works at Hungry's. He saw her that morning, too, and his story makes sense so far. The other is Dr. Flammarion."

Harvey Mitchum frowned and put his feet up again. "Flammarion?"

"The Knights hired him as their personal apothecary. He's injected the Knights with so much laudanum they're scarcely aware their daughter is missing."

"So what?" Mimi said. "The Knight family's medical care is their own business, and if their spoiled teenage daughter wants to join the circus, there's nothing we can do about it."

"She's a brilliant chemist, not a spoiled

teenager," I said. "If she'd run away, she would have left a note for everyone in that household who loved her."

"Maybe," Harvey said.

"Maybe," I agreed. "And maybe the law ought to investigate a missing girl."

"How can we do that?"

"You could get the idea to go ask Dr. Flammarion some tough questions about Cleo Knight's disappearance."

Mimi stood up straight and pushed her husband's feet off the desk again. "I've just had an idea," she said. "Let's go ask Dr. Flammarion some questions about Cleo Knight's disappearance."

"Some *tough* questions," her husband agreed.

"Of course the questions will be tough, Harvey. What did you think I meant—go ask him some easy questions?"

"How should I know what you mean? You talk nonsense half the time."

"Well, you talk nonsense two-thirds of the time."

"There's no way you can calculate something like that."

"Can we go with you, Officers?" Moxie asked, snapping her typewriter shut.

"Absolutely not," Harvey Mitchum said. "Stay away from this case. That goes for you too, Snicket. I appreciate your bringing this matter to our attention, but from now on this investigation will be carried out in an orderly and mature way. Stewart, I'll need you to make your siren noise."

"Of course, Daddy dear," Stew said, and we all walked out of the station. Mimi Mitchum shut and locked the door, and Stew took the opportunity to extend his foot in hopes of tripping me as we walked down the stairs. Moxie had seen this trick before, and swung her typewriter low and hard against Stew's knee. He howled loudly. She apologized sweetly. He was still howling when the Mitchums led him across the lawn.

"That was a nice trick, Moxie," I said, "with the typewriter."

"So was yours," she said, "with the haircut. Are you really going to stay away from this case?"

"Of course not," I said. "It's my job to find Cleo Knight."

"What is this job, exactly?" she asked. "Who do you work for? Where did you come from? How long will you stay? When will you leave? Why are you investigating things in this town?"

"It's a complicated story," I said.

"I have time and I have a typewriter," Moxie said. "Tell me the whole thing."

I took a deep breath of fresh air. I thought of my sister, who was probably deep underground, far from even the smallest breeze. "In my line of work," I said, "people who learn the whole thing tend to end up in grave danger. I don't want to lead you into the same predicament."

Moxie cocked her head at me, and her brown hat cocked along with her. "Then where are you going to lead me, Lemony Snicket?" she asked.

"Not far," I said, and I walked to the other side of the building to the library door.

CHAPTER SIX

A library tends to look like the problem you're using it to solve. The library of Stain'd-by-the-Sea had never looked so big and confusing to me. The books and shelves seemed to be in the middle of an argument nobody was winning.

"Apologies for the mess." It was the deep voice of Dashiell Qwerty, but I couldn't see him anywhere. His desk was towered with books, with a few of his eternal enemies—a phrase which here means "moths"—fluttering just out of the reach of his checkered handkerchief. "We've had some recent concerns, so the library is taking some precautionary measures."

"What concerns?" Moxie asked, already opening her typewriter. "What measures?"

Qwerty moved a few books aside so he could face us. He called himself a sub-librarian, but I considered him to be not only a proper librarian but a good and proper librarian. He was dressed in his usual leather jacket decorated with pieces of metal, and his hair as usual looked frightened of it. "A few books have gone missing," he said, "and there have been some threats."

"Who made the threats?"

"I wish I knew," he said. "In any case, I'm completely reorganizing the shelves, and in a few days a sprinkler system will be installed so we don't have to worry about fire. In the meantime, if you're looking for a good book to read, allow me to recommend a book I like called *Despair*. The plot concerns two people who do not look at all alike but nevertheless hatch a nefarious plan."

"It sounds interesting," I said, "although my associate and I have a number of things to research."

Qwerty gave me a familiar smile and made a wide gesture with his hand and the sleeve of his leather jacket. I liked the gesture. It was not like Theodora's dramatic gestures, which seemed designed to make you look at her. This was a gesture designed to make you look around the library, and I liked what he always said when the gesture was through. "Make yourself at home," he said, and Moxie and I shared a smile and thanked him and headed off down the crowded aisles.

"So?" she said, when we were out of earshot.

"So this is where I do my research."

"Yes, but what are we researching?"

"Dr. Flammarion is obviously up to something," I said, "and we need to find out what it is."

"There's not going to be a book on Dr. Flammarion," Moxie said.

"No," I said, "but there might be one about Colonel Colophon."

"What does he have to do with all this?"

"I wish I knew," I admitted. "He was Ingrid Nummet Knight's business partner, and Dr. Flammarion works at the clinic where the colonel lives. I also want to do some research on chemistry. Dr. Flammarion works with laudanum, and Cleo Knight was working with invisible ink. Maybe there's another connection there."

"I'll tackle Colonel Colophon, and you take chemistry. Fair?"

"Fair."

"And Snicket?"

"Yes, Moxie?"

"Do you really consider me an associate?"

"Certainly."

She smiled the way people smile when they

are trying to stop smiling. "So we're solving this case together?"

"I told you before I don't want to lead you into danger," I said. "We don't know what happened to Cleo Knight."

"If it's safe enough for you, it's safe enough for me," Moxie said firmly.

"I was trained for this sort of thing," I said. "It was part of my education."

"Is Theodora part of this education?"

"Yes," I said. "She's my associate, too."

"The same Theodora who made you steal the Bombinating Beast from me? The same Theodora who thinks that no crime was committed in this case?" The journalist put down her typewriter on one of the library's desks. "I might be a better associate than your associate."

Moxie Mallahan was reminding me of me. I was known for arguing with my teachers until they became so flustered they could think of only one thing to say to me. It was an unfair thing, the thing they said, but I was almost thirteen. I was used to unfair things. "Let's get to work," I told her.

Moxie sighed and walked away from me, toward the section of the library dedicated to military history. I headed toward Science, hoping that the books I was looking for would be on the shelves and not in the messy stacks that clogged the aisles. To get to the Science Section, I had to walk through Fiction, where there was a gap, three books wide, blank and obvious like a missing tooth. It was my fault. I had found it necessary to remove three books from the library without checking them out, and now the books were in Hangfire's possession. They were good books, and now nobody could check them out. Don't mope about it, Snicket. There's nothing you can do.

The Science Section was in no order whatsoever, so chemistry books were piled with biology books stacked with botany books leaned up against endocrinology. I sighed, but it didn't get any better. The room was quiet. I knelt on the ground and began to look through everything. There wasn't a book called *Laudanum* or a book called *Invisible Ink* or a book called *Laudanum and Invisible Ink* or a book called *The Case of Cleo Knight's Disappearance Solved in a Book So Lemony Snicket Doesn't Have to Do It Himself.* I did find a book about chemistry, but I didn't want to read it. It was as big as a cake and it was called *Chemistry.* It had no index, so there was no way to look in the back of the book to see where the sections on laudanum were. You had to stumble on them. I wanted to stumble on whoever had made the decision not to put an index in the back of *Chemistry.* I lugged it to a table and started reading.

Chemistry is a branch of science dealing with the basic elementary substances of which all bodies and matter are composed, and the laws that regulate the combination of these elements when forming compounds, and the phenomena that occur when such bodies are exposed to differing physical conditions and environments. I closed the book. I had read enough. Cleo Knight would die peacefully in her sleep at age 102, surrounded by her great-grandchildren, before this book would help me with the case.

I allowed myself a moment of melancholy instead. It was late afternoon. Just a moment, I told myself. Just one moment of melancholy. I thought of my sister, in a tunnel underneath the city. It would be dark there, although she would likely have a lantern or a torch. She would frown in the way she does when she is concentrating very hard. She is measuring her steps, making sure that she ends up directly under the Museum of Items. Then I thought of my parents. I thought of how they looked in the shade of a tall tree, one long-ago afternoon. The wind was blowing hard, and we were foolishly hiking. The wind caught a heavy branch of a tree and sent it tumbling down. You could hear it coming, thrashing through the leaves, for what seemed like a long time. My mother leapt—a great, long, surprising leap—and blocked the branch with her arms, sending it rolling into the underbrush. I remembered the sound. She had been just in time. "We take care of our own," my mother said, while my sister and my brother and I all stood gaping at the branch that would have ruined our day. "We Snickets take care of our own."

I was not taking care of our own. My sister was alone, and I was in a library indulging in melancholy. Indulging means doing something that is really not necessary. I stood up and found Moxie.

"What does 'teetotaler' mean?" she asked me.

"A person who doesn't drink alcohol," I said.

"Colonel Colophon is a teetotaler," she said, "although I can't imagine that will help us any more than anything else. He fought bravely

115

in the war, but I got sidetracked a little reading about that. I thought the war was a simple matter, with one side good and the other evil. But the more I read, the less clear it was."

"I think that's true of all wars."

"Maybe. In any case, the town of Stain'd-by-the-Sea honored him with that statue. Here they are at the groundbreaking ceremony."

She turned the book around on the desk, and I looked at a large photograph of a crowd. The caption told me that politicians, artists, scientists, tycoons, naturalists, veterans, and other citizens were gathering in front of City Hall for the first day of work on the statue honoring Colonel Colophon. The place looked a lot better in the photograph than it did now. The pillars were smooth and the lawn well tended, and there was a tall, broad tree, about to be cut down, where they were going to erect the statue. Stop thinking about trees, Snicket. Stop thinking about your family. There were several men and women in firefighter uniforms, and there was a small brass band from the Wade Academy, which was once a top-drawer school but now sat empty and abandoned just outside town on Offshore Island. I thought I saw the Officers Mitchum in the crowd, looking much younger, and there was Prosper Lost, rubbing his hands together. There was a young woman who looked like she might have been Polly Partial, some years ago, and there was a man who looked like he might have been Dr. Flammarion, beardless and laughing with a group of other men and women. Of course, most people in the crowd were unknown to me. Some of them looked happy, and some of them didn't. I didn't know why I was looking at them.

"Is there anything about what happened later?" I asked. "What about the explosion?"

"There's not much," Moxie said. "As far as I can tell, Colonel Colophon spends all his time in the Colophon Clinic, holed up in his special attic hospital room or wandering the grounds. See, here's a photograph of him sitting by the clinic's swimming pool."

"He really does look like a mummy."

"A mummy on the back of a monster. Take a good look at that bench."

I took a good look at the bench where the colonel was sitting. The Bombinating Beast, Stain'd-by-the-Sea's legendary monster, stared back at me from the photograph.

"It looks like that bench is made from the same wood as the statue Hangfire's after," Moxie said.

"Same wood, same beast. There must be a connection."

"If there is, I can't find it. Or there might be something, but I missed it because the library is in such disarray."

"Do you think the newsroom in the light-house might have some old articles about all this?"

"It's possible," Moxie said, "but *The Stain'd Lighthouse* is in disarray, too. Many issues of the newspaper have gone missing. My mother took some when she left town, and I'm afraid my father doesn't do a very good job of looking after things."

"You must miss her."

"Every minute, Snicket, of every hour of every day. What about you? What did you find?"

"Chemistry is a branch of science dealing with the basic elementary substances of which all bodies and matter are composed, and the laws that regulate—"

Moxie held up her hands. "Boredom is not black licorice, Snicket," she said. "There's no reason to share it with me."

"I think I'll ask the librarian for help," I said. "He's busy, but he's good."

"I'll type up a few more notes," Moxie said, and I nodded and headed toward the librarian's desk. At first I thought that Dashiell Qwerty had left the library, as I thought I caught a shadow across the door, but then I saw him brushing the spine of a fancy-looking book on oysters, using a soft, thick brush and fierce concentration.

"Excuse me," I said, "but I haven't found what I'm looking for."

"A common complaint."

"I need information on laudanum, or other sleeping draughts, or a history of chemical espionage, and anything on Colonel Colophon and the explosion that wounded him and the clinic founded in his honor."

"You would do well to be less particular," Qwerty said, waving away a moth. "With a library it is easier to hope for serendipity than to look for a precise answer."

"Serendipity?"

"Serendipity is a happy accident," Qwerty said. "In a library, that could mean finding something you didn't know you were looking for. In any case, I'm afraid most of the books covering the subjects you mentioned have been checked out. A cardholder reserved them some time ago and picked them up just now."

I blinked, and then hurried to the door. The shadow I had seen was no longer a shadow. Now it was a woman, walking down the steps toward the lawn where once there had been a tall, broad tree. Then there had been a statue. Now there were the remains of a statue. The woman was wearing a white coat that looked official and made me nervous. I didn't recognize her. She was carrying a load of books under one arm and a bag of groceries in the other. I could see into the top of the bag. It looked like she'd bought some milk, a loaf of bread, and perhaps a dozen lemons. And then there was a tall box of something you might have for breakfast, if you liked twelve wholesome grains combined in strict sequence.

"Who is that?" I asked Qwerty, trying to keep

my voice quiet. "Who checked out those books?"

"A librarian doesn't reveal information like that," Qwerty replied. "Who you are and what you read is private in a library. The world—"

"I tell you, I must know who that is," I said.

Qwerty put a hand on my shoulder. The metal decorations jangled on the sleeves of his jacket. "And I tell you," he said gently, "that you will not get that information from me."

I looked again at the departing woman, and then at Qwerty, and then all around the library, with its wild stacks of books. There were three new ones now, stacked right on the desk. The woman had returned three books to the library, three books that fit perfectly into a gap in Fiction. I had slipped those books out of the library, and now they were back again. It shouldn't have been surprising. Of course Hangfire was involved in some way.

The three books were all by the same author, and I recommend all three of them. There is one about a girl who spies on her neighbors and one about creepy notes that ruin people's summer and one about a family that does not change even though the children want it to. They had been in Hangfire's possession, which meant that the woman who returned them was one of his associates. I could not get any information about her by asking a librarian, but there was another way. I took one last look around the library and hurried after her.

CHAPTER SEVEN

The woman walking through the streets of Stain'd-by-the-Sea, carrying a bag of groceries and a stack of books, had her hair coiled up on her head like a cobra in a basket. You could tell her feet hurt. You could tell that when she was angry, she knew just the thing to say to make you squirm. She passed Diceys Department Store, with its quiet, sad mannequins in the windows. She passed Ink Inc., with its little closed door. I kept behind her. She didn't look back once. The trick to following someone without getting caught is to follow somebody who doesn't think they're being followed. This is how I learned to follow people, and over the course of an entire school year, I learned fascinating secrets about complete strangers I followed for hours on end. It made me wonder who knew my secrets, on the days I thought I was walking with no one behind me.

She turned the corner and I waited a little before following her onto a quiet block. There was not even a single business, no Hungry's or Lost Arms or Black Cat Coffee. Once upon a time it must have been a pretty block, I thought. There would have been shops, instead of smashed windows and chained doors, and above the shops were rows of apartments that would have been occupied. Each apartment had tall windows and balconies that were broken and deserted. It was easy to imagine how they might have looked on a hot day, with the windows flung open and people on the balconies sipping cool drinks and staring down at a parade that might be going by—a parade for a military hero, for instance. I thought of Colonel Colophon, and the statue in front of the library. It was like a tune I couldn't stop humming but couldn't name either. It fit somehow. I should have taken a better look at the photograph Moxie showed me. Moxie will be as mad as a paper cut, I thought, when she notices I've left the library without her. Stop it, Snicket. Focus on the woman in front of you, frowning into each doorway. Her shoes look like she stepped in something wet and dirty. The doorways are all boarded up. She won't find anything there.

She rounded another corner. I had to wait. The street was so quiet, but when I peeked around the corner, it was quieter still.

The woman was gone.

I forced myself to calm down. If someone disappears around a corner, it means they've gone into one of the buildings or a giant bird has carried them away. The skies were clear, so I checked doorways. There was an abandoned restaurant, with round tables that were too small to eat at comfortably. I peered through the cracked window and read some words on a chalkboard—LES GOMMES, which was French for who knew what—but the door was nailed shut, tight as a coffin. Before long all doors in town would be that way, with the Knights abandoning their ink business and moving to the city.

Across the street was another closed business. The broken sign read UARIU, which didn't look like French. The windows were covered in black cloth, like someone had drawn curtains. The door was shut, but there was something fluttering under it, stuck in the crack where the door tried to meet the ground. It was white, a single piece of paper. I walked over and tugged on the corner of it. It slid out of the door.

MISSING, it read. It was one of the posters

for Cleo Knight. If it was stuck in the door, that meant the door had been opened recently. Perhaps just moments before.

I dropped the flyer and it flew, the wind carrying it down the street in a hurry. I reminded myself of a lesson I'd learned in my training: Do the scary thing first, and get scared later.

I pushed at the door and it creaked slightly. I would have to open it very slowly. A little creak here, a little creak there. Probably no one would hear it. Because probably no one would be anywhere near the door. They would be far, far from the door, whoever they were. And they would be happy to see me if I happened to pop in. So why are you waiting outside, I asked myself. Get scared later.

I pushed the door open, slow as long division. The door creaked, but I was the only one listening. The floor was wet and dirty, but there was nobody there. I was inside the shop, or what had been a shop. I was right. "UARIU" wasn't French.

It was most of the word "AQUARIUM." Once the people of Stain'd-by-the-Sea had come here to buy fish and bowls and all of the equipment to care for them. Perhaps some of the fish had come from just off the shores of the town, when it was still sea rather than the lawless landscape of the Clusterous Forest. But now the fish were gone. A few cracked tanks sat dirty on shelves, but most had been taken away. Containers of food, and little plastic castles that people enjoy thinking fish enjoy, were forgotten in piles. The only sign of life was a solitary bowl placed on the dusty counter next to a dusty cash register and an empty coffee mug. Inside were a handful of what looked like tiny black tadpoles, swimming in murky water. There was a chunk of something pale green for them to nibble on, and a large chunk of wood that rose up at an angle, as if to give the tadpoles something to climb. I peered at the tadpoles, but they showed no interest.

There was a trail of footprints across the muddy floor and through an open door in the back to a dark staircase leading up. But I already knew where the woman had gone. I could hear her footsteps overhead. I thought for a minute and grabbed the mug before going quietly up the stairs. The tadpoles didn't watch me go. They had other thoughts.

The stairs stopped at the door to an apartment, as I thought they would, and then curved on upstairs to another apartment. There wasn't a welcome mat, but I wouldn't have felt welcome anyway. I held the mug up to the door, with the open side next to the wood, and then pressed my ear to the other side. An empty glass works better, or a stethoscope if you have one handy, but nobody has a stethoscope handy.

"I bought all the lemons at the supermarket," the woman was saying, and I heard her *thunk* down her bag, a loud sound over another, fainter one.

"Thank you," said another voice. It was the

voice of a girl. "You can put the lemons in the refrigerator, along with the milk. I'll chop them up later."

"You'll do no such thing," the woman said, and I heard the lemons roll out onto a table.

"Well, at least let me help you," the girl said. "You're doing so much work, Nurse Dander."

"And you're not doing any," Nurse Dander said sourly. I heard the high-pitched sound of metal scraping against metal, and then a sequence of noises in a strict row: *Chunk-rattle! Chunk-rattle! Chunk-rattle! Chunk-rattle!* "I thought you'd need all sorts of scientific equipment," she said. *Chunk-rattle! Chunk-rattle!* "But you've just set up a bunch of bowls and glasses from the kitchen. It looks like cooking, not chemistry."

"Cooking is a lot like chemistry," the girl said. The voice felt a bit wrong. I couldn't exactly say how. It was a high voice, except on certain words when it was suddenly quite low. Some of the words came out almost too clearly and some were all muttery, as if she were chewing on a marble.

"I hope so," the nurse said. *Chunk-rattle! Chunk-rattle! Chunk-rattle!* "He'll expect results. And quickly!"

"Has he been here?"

"That's none of your business." *Chunk-rattle! Chunk-rattle!*

"I think he has."

"He goes wherever he wants, whenever he wants." *Chunk-rattle! Chunk-rattle!* "And the next time he's back here, he'll expect you to have what you promised."

"And when will that be?" asked the girl.

"I told you, that's none of your business." *Chunk-rattle! Chunk-rattle! Chunk-rattle! Chunk-rattle!* "There, that's the lot of them. You can squeeze the lemons yourself."

"You're good with a knife."

"You remember that if you ever try to escape."

"I won't," the girl promised.

"You'd better not," Nurse Dander said. "You have everything you need now. Get to work."

"Couldn't we talk for a minute?"

"We have just talked for a minute."

"But I like the company."

"We're not friends. You're working for us. I've brought you everything you asked for. You said lemons. Many lemons, you said. Certain books, you said."

"Well, I hope it works," said the girl uncertainly, "but it might not. During this season the lemon juice has considerably less…"

The voice trailed off, and I could hear Nurse Dander's fingernails rattling impatiently on something. The fainter sound, I realized, was music. "Less what?"

"Less of an important chemical."

"What chemical?"

Beekabackabooka, I thought.

"One that's crucial for the work I'm doing," the voice said, even higher and lower than usual.

The woman's footsteps moved slowly, slowly, slowly across the room. "You are here on your honor, Cleo Knight. Do not cross us. We are not a Society that tolerates treachery. We've given you everything you asked for. It's time for you to uphold your promise as well."

"Could you at least pass a message to Hangfire?"

For a second there was no sound at all, and I shivered against the mug. Then the woman spoke very quietly. "I told you never to mention his name," she said, and there was the sound of metal against metal once more. I could not tell if the woman was putting away the knife or pointing it at the girl. "Don't provoke me."

The footsteps came toward me. There was nowhere to go and no time to go there, so I did the only thing I could think of, which was nothing. The door opened and pushed me to the wall. It smelled bad. My hand gripped the handle of the mug. When the door swung back

135

I would be discovered, except the door didn't swing back. "Provoke" means to irritate someone so much that they might not notice what is going on around them. Nurse Dander stomped up the stairs past me. I did not get a good look at her. I did not see if she had the knife. My eyes were closed. It is useless to close your eyes when you are hiding, but everyone does it anyway. I reminded myself to breathe, and myself thanked me as the door slammed shut. The girl locked it. I was alone. You cannot be sure, I told myself. You cannot know what you hope you know.

I knocked on the door.

"Yes?" The voice of the girl forgot for a moment what it should sound like, but then it remembered its wrong sound. "Who is it?"

"Delivery," I said, also using a fake voice, "for Miss Cleo Knight."

"There is no one here by that name," the voice replied.

"Perhaps I should try upstairs," I said.

"No!" I could hear the girl's hands scurry around the lock, making sure I couldn't get in. "There's no one in the building named Cleo Knight!"

"I'm sorry," I said. "I misread the label. It's a different name."

"What name?"

I said the first name that came to mind.

"There's no one here by that name either."

"I wouldn't think so. It's the name of an author from Sweden."

I heard the hands around the lock again, but slower this time.

"She wrote a book about a girl with a long name and long braids who has adventures with her neighbors. It's more interesting to have adventures with other people, don't you think?"

The voice didn't say anything.

"I mean, you wouldn't want to be alone if you were in dangerous circumstances."

The voice saw no reason to break its silence.

"There are other books about her, too. There's one where she goes to the South Seas. Doesn't that sound fun?"

"Go away," the voice said, very quietly.

"You're not very good at disguising your voice."

"Neither are you."

"This is asinine," I said. "Open the door."

"Asinine" is a word that sounds like you shouldn't say it, so when you do say it, people often gasp. This makes it a delicious way of saying "not very smart," which is all it means. There was no gasp from the other side of the door, but the lock clicked and the door opened and I walked inside.

It was a shabby apartment. There was a badly leaning lamp and a long wooden table someone had pounded with something. Now it was covered in bowls and glasses, with a stack of books at one end, and a great number of lemons, all cut in half. There was a large pile of papers on a rickety chair, and there was a sofa piled with lumpy pillows and ugly blankets, for someone to sleep, or try to sleep. The only handsome thing in the room was a small box with a crank on its side and a funnel on top, with music coming out of it. And there was a girl standing in front of me. Her green eyes were the same, but her hair wasn't black, not now. It was blond instead, so blond it looked white. Her fingers were still slender, with long black nails again, and over her eyes were strange eyebrows curved like question marks. She was using the same smile, too. It was a smile I liked. It was a smile that might have meant anything.

Now you can be sure, I told myself. Now you have found her and now you can say her name.

"Ellington Feint."

CHAPTER EIGHT

"Lemony Snicket," she said right back to me. We stood and faced each other. I hadn't known Ellington Feint very long, and you couldn't quite say that we were friends. We both found ourselves in Stain'd-by-the-Sea on mysterious errands. We had both stolen the same statue, and we were both searching for the same villain, and now the Cleo Knight case had thrown us together again. But the Bombinating Beast, fashioned after Stain'd-by-the-Sea's legendary monster, and Hangfire, who was holding Ellington's father prisoner, and even the disappearance of a brilliant chemist didn't make us friends. We were more like jigsaw pieces, each of us parts of the same big picture. There are people like this wherever you go. They are part of the same mystery as you are, but you can't quite tell how you fit together. The world is a puzzle, and we cannot solve it alone.

"What are you doing here, Ms. Feint?" I said.

"I might ask you the same question, Mr. Snicket."

"I'm looking for Cleo Knight," I said.

Ellington moved now, and quickly shut the door. "As far as everyone here is concerned," she said in a whisper, "I *am* Cleo Knight."

I sat down at the table with all the kitchen equipment and the lemons sliced in half. I had most of the story, but not all of it. "That's quite a stunt," I said. "How did you do it?"

Ellington walked to the sofa and reached underneath it to pull out a suitcase. It was the one she'd carried with her from Killdeer Fields, the nearby town where she had grown up. It was filled with all sorts of clothing—everything she needed to wear on her journey to find her father. She held up a new coat with black and white stripes, and a hat the color of a raspberry.

"The hat I remember," I said. "I saw it when you were living in Handkerchief Heights. Where did you get the coat?"

"Cleo Knight bought it for me," she said, "at Diceys Department Store."

"That's a generous gift. You must be very good friends."

"I wouldn't call us friends," Ellington said. "I only met her a few weeks ago, at Black Cat Coffee. She was trying to get the machine to make her a cup of tea to help her think. I convinced her to try coffee instead, and we started to talk. She told me that her parents were abandoning the ink business and moving to the city, but she has been working on an important experiment that could save the town."

"Invisible ink," I said.

Ellington smiled. "I should have known you would know. Cleo Knight really is a brilliant chemist. Usually, invisible ink is just some nonsense with lemon juice, but she's almost perfected a new formula, with a secret ingredient she discovered herself. There will be invisible inkwells everywhere, she told me, just as soon as the formula is finished. People will go back to work. Stain'd-by-the-Sea will thrive again. The octopi will no longer be endangered. They could even put the sea back where it belongs, all because of Cleo Knight's formula. Can you imagine? Invisible ink that actually works."

"There are certain people I know who would be very interested in that," I said.

"S. Theodora Markson, your chaperone, for instance?"

"Any number of people would be interested in invisible ink that actually works."

"That's exactly what Cleo Knight was worried about. She didn't want her formula to fall into the wrong hands."

"She was right to worry," I said, thinking of Dr. Flammarion.

"And she was right to disappear. She knew danger was nearby. Her parents had been very supportive of her experiments, but then suddenly they began acting strangely and insisted on leaving town. It was a desperate situation, Snicket. The fate of the entire town was in the hands of Cleo Knight. So we made a deal."

"You gave her your extra hat," I said, "and she bought you an extra coat."

"She even found me the right chemical to make my hair blond."

"So now there were two Cleo Knights."

"The real Cleo Knight found a safe place to hide, left a note for her parents, and drove off in her fancy car with her special equipment. And I'm supposed to pop up around town dressed like her, talking about joining the circus, so if anyone goes looking for her, they'll be on the wrong track."

"And then?"

Ellington smiled, but she wasn't looking at me. "And then nothing," she said. "That's the whole story. Cleo Knight is somewhere safe, working on her experiments, and I'm confusing her enemies until she's done."

"That's not the whole story," I said, "not by a long shot. First of all, her family never found a note, and Cleo Knight and her Dilemma never made it to any safe place. Someone changed the plan, Ms. Feint. Someone destroyed the note and kept Mr. and Mrs. Knight in a state of unhurried delirium, thanks to regular injections of laudanum. And someone gave the Dilemma a flat tire with a hypodermic needle and then offered Cleo Knight a ride. Someone she trusted—the family's private apothecary, Dr. Flammarion."

"I don't know him."

"Maybe not, Ms. Feint. But the woman in the apartment above this one—the woman taking care of you—is Dr. Flammarion's nurse."

Ellington looked up at the apartment's flickering chandelier, as if she expected the woman to drop through the ceiling. "How did you know?"

"I followed her from the library," I said. "She returned some books that I hadn't seen in some time—books that were in the possession of Hangfire. That villain is controlling everything, Ellington. Remember when he forced Dame Sally Murphy to impersonate Mrs. Murphy Sallis? Now Hangfire has Dr. Flammarion doing his dirty work. He has Nurse Dander helping him. And he has you too, Ms. Feint."

"What do you mean?"

"Nurse Dander said you were here on your honor. She said you needed to uphold your promise. You're doing something for them, Ms. Feint.

You're helping Hangfire with his treachery, and you don't even know it!"

Now she looked at me. Her eyes seemed greener, or perhaps the green was just more angry than I had seen green before. She pointed one furious finger at me, her fingernails as black as the nights in the Far East Suite, when it was very, very late and I still couldn't fall asleep. "Of course I know it, Mr. Snicket," she said. "Do you think I came to this place by accident? When I was in the attic of Black Cat Coffee, I found a package. It was addressed to my father, in care of an organization I had never heard of."

She reached into a pocket and pulled out a badly wrinkled label, which she spread out on the table. Together we frowned at it.

ARMSTRONG FEINT C/O THE INHUMANE SOCIETY

There was no more to the address. There had been quite a few packages the last time I was in that attic. I hadn't thought of them as clues. "What's the Inhumane Society?" I said.

Ellington's eyebrows gave me their best curl. "You don't know?" she said. "I thought you were a member, Mr. Snicket."

"No," I said carefully. "My organization is different."

For a second neither of us said anything, although our secrets were arguing in the air above us. "I stayed in that attic for two days," she said finally. "I came out of hiding only to eat bread and drink coffee."

"Where did you hide?" I asked.

"There's a cupboard," she said, "that's larger than it looks."

"I looked for you over and over."

"I know you did, Mr. Snicket," she said. "I kept thinking you were going to pick up the package."

"You think I know where your father is?"

Ellington did not smile, but she looked like she had thought of smiling. "We're not exactly friends, Mr. Snicket," she said. "You just dropped into a tree one evening, and ever since, I've had the feeling that we're part of the same mystery."

I did not like to think about my ridiculous fall into a tree, though I often thought about Ellington finding me there and bringing me down. "I promised I would help you find him," I reminded her. "If I knew where he was, I would tell you."

She gave me a small nod. "In any case, it wasn't you who picked up the package. It was Nurse Dander. I followed her here, but I was afraid to go further. The abandoned aquarium looked so eerie, and I didn't know what I would find inside. But when I met Cleo Knight and we cooked up our plan, I knew I had my chance. Instead of popping up all over town, I made just one appearance, at Partial Foods. Then I took a taxi here and knocked on the door. Nurse Dander answered, and I introduced myself as Cleo Knight. I promised a formula for invisible ink that actually worked, in exchange for a meeting with Hangfire. It's a good plan, Mr. Snicket."

"Oh sure," I said, "like juggling dynamite, or kicking a polar bear."

"Don't be asinine."

"What's asinine is trying to trick a villain like that."

"It's the only way," Ellington said. "I went to all that trouble of getting the Bombinating Beast, but when I left him a message telling him I had it, he never answered. I need to rescue my father, Mr. Snicket. Pleasing Hangfire is the only way."

I did not mention that the one who had gone to all that trouble to get the statue was me. I did not ask her how she left a message for Hangfire. When I sit and think of this incident in my life, beginning with the phone call from my sister and ending in the basement of the Colophon Clinic, the list of things I did wrong stretches out in front of me and I cannot see the end of it. "You can't make invisible ink, can you?"

"Of course not," Ellington said, with a helpless

gesture at everything on the table. "I don't even know what the secret additive is. When Nurse Dander is here, I putter around pretending to be a scientist. And when she goes out, I search the building for my father."

"What have you found?"

"Nothing. Nurse Dander's apartment is ordinary, and the rest of the apartments are empty. It's a mystery why there's furniture in this one. I haven't seen Hangfire, but I think he's been here."

"How could you know? You've never seen him."

"It's just a feeling I have," she said, looking across the shabby room.

"Someone else will get a feeling too, Ms. Feint. Someone will get a feeling that you're tricking them."

"But everyone thinks I'm Cleo Knight, the brilliant scientist. Everyone trusts her."

"But the real Cleo Knight is in Hangfire's

clutches," I said. "He will tell Dr. Flammarion, and Dr. Flammarion will tell his nurse. And his nurse is good with a knife."

Ellington looked at me now. Her eyes widened beneath her eyebrows, and her fingers curled up like talons on the table. We both stared up at the chandelier, listening for any sound from Nurse Dander's apartment. But all we heard was the record Ellington was playing. It wasn't a tune I knew. I could hear a trumpet and a trombone, with a piano and some drums tapping along. It sounded carefree. Everyone was having fun, wherever they were where the music was happening. "What do I do?" she asked me quietly.

"Don't get scared now," I said. "You are a marvel of a girl, Ms. Feint. You follow people in the street and disguise yourself as a brilliant chemist. You knock on the doors of villains and trick them. If you were in that Swedish book, it would say you could whip your weight in wildcats."

"Actually, wildcats frighten me. My father

and I saw one once on a hike, and it still gives me nightmares."

"I tell stories too," I said, "when I'm nervous. We need to get out of here, Ms. Feint. Leave everything behind, particularly the library books on chemistry. They're boring."

"How can I leave?" Ellington said. "Nurse Dander will hear me."

"She can hear you," I said, "but she can't know you're you."

"She's seen all these clothes," Ellington said. "She searched my suitcase when I got here."

I took off my coat. "She hasn't searched me," I said. "Take this."

"The sun is going down," she said. "It's cold outside, Mr. Snicket."

"So I'll shiver," I said. "I've shivered before."

She looked down at the table and traced her father's name with a black fingernail. "So have I," she said, and put on my coat. She rummaged in the suitcase for a few hairpins and in moments had her long hair pinned up on top of her head. It felt private to watch her do that. I had never seen my sister or my mother when they did whatever they did to their hair. It was a secret.

"What do you think, Mr. Snicket? Do I look like a boy?"

"No. From a distance, maybe."

"How is this going to work?"

"It's easy," I said. "I learned how to do it."

"From your organization."

"Yes," I said.

Ellington looked around the room. "I don't like leaving these things behind."

"Which things do you mean?"

"My phonograph. My papers. And..."

The music kept at it.

"Don't worry, Ms. Feint," I said, when the pause was over. "I'll bring it to you. We can't be seen leaving together, and you shouldn't have it with you, in case you're caught. But I'll take it out of here, and I'll meet you."

"Where?"

"You know where. Corner of Caravan and Parfait."

"You promise?"

"I promise. But you'd better show me where it is."

I liked that Ellington didn't even pretend not to know what I meant. She walked over to the refrigerator and opened it. It was the sort that had a few drawers, called crispers. She opened one, and inside nothing was very crisp. It looked like lettuce, or something that had been lettuce during a happier time. Now it was slimy and watery and looked like nothing you'd want to touch, which I suppose was the idea. Ellington brushed the old lettuce aside and withdrew something large and black. It looked something like a sea horse, with small holes for eyes, and a nasty, hollow smile. I didn't know what it was before, and I didn't know what it was then. The statue gave me a look like it wasn't going to tell me. I held it in my hands and turned it over for a minute to feel the patch of crinkly paper that was pasted over a small slit. Spend some time with me, I thought. Sit with me, you terrible beast. Tell me all your secrets. But there wasn't time, not then. I took the smallest blanket from the sofa, light blue with silly fringes on the edges, and wrapped up the beast so no one would see what I was carrying.

"Take good care of that," she said.

"What is it, exactly?" I asked her.

She gave me a tiny shrug. "It's my only hope," she said, and I walked her to the door. I looked at her and wanted to tell her to take good care of something, too. But I wasn't quite sure what it was, so I opened the door very quietly and then knocked on it very loudly.

"Delivery," I said, in my "delivery" voice. "Delivery for Miss Cleo Knight."

Ellington caught on at once. "Sir," she said

sternly, "I told you there is no one here by that name or any other name either."

"My mistake," I said. "See you later."

"See you later," she replied, and with one last look at me, she hurried down the stairs just as I heard from overhead the sound of another door opening.

"Miss Knight?" Nurse Dander called down to me. "Who was that? Was someone looking for you?"

I didn't answer, of course. I couldn't imitate voices. I was no Hangfire. But neither did I want Nurse Dander to think there was no one in the apartment. I walked quickly to the record player and turned up the volume. The musicians sounded even happier. Ellington was right. It was a shame to leave something like that behind.

"Miss Knight?" the nurse called again.

I looked around quickly. The bathroom, I thought. Even the shabbiest of apartments has a bathroom. I walked through the only doorway I could see, and found myself in a very tiny bathroom, made tinier by a sink so large there was room for a goldfish bowl on the rim. The bowl had nothing but a small black tadpole, like the one I had seen in the aquarium, with another chunk of food and another chunk of wood in case it was in a climbing mood. It didn't appear to be. The faucet was dripping steadily, but I wasn't going to fix it. I drew back the shower curtain and saw a small window, open just a crack. The air whistled through the crack and reminded me of something. It was not big enough to climb out of.

"Miss Knight, answer me!"

I put the statue, still wrapped in a blanket, down on the dirty tiles of the floor. A distraction, I thought. A loud noise. Out the window. Enough time for Ellington to escape and for you to get out, too. Yes, I must find a weight or some other heavy object. Something in the kitchen. But Nurse Dander was already walking down the stairs, and then I heard her step into the apartment. She had a slight wheeze I had not noticed before. I could hear it now, because she was so close to me.

"Miss Knight?" she said.

I listened to her wheezing and put the stopper in the sink. The faucet kept dripping. I stepped into the shower and slowly, slowly opened the window all the way.

"Miss Knight?" Nurse Dander said one more time, like a warning, and then I heard that high-pitched sound again, of metal scraping against metal. Good with a knife means nothing, I said to myself. It's just an expression. Think of another expression. The cat's pajamas, that's a funny one. Why should it mean something wonderful, what a cat wears to bed? Get scared later.

There was enough water in the sink now. I leaned over the fishbowl. There was a sweet smell, the smell of something I didn't like. Forget it, Snicket. You do not see the point of honeydew

melons. I reached in and quickly cupped the tadpole in my hand. I lifted it out and dropped it into the sink, but my finger hurt just as I did, a sharp and angry pain, like I'd been stuck with a piece of glass. But it isn't broken yet, Snicket.

"Where are you, Knight?"

I looked at my finger. It was bleeding, just a tiny bit. *Bit.* I had been bitten. I glared down at the tadpole. I was trying to save you, and you bite me, you ungrateful tiny thing? It ignored me. It was busy circling its new surroundings. I picked up the fishbowl and stepped back into the shower. Now the voice was at the door.

"Knight?"

I heaved the fishbowl out the window and for a second listened to nothing. Then I listened to a terrific crash of glass. It was very loud. It made me grin. Everyone in the neighborhood could hear it, but I only cared about one person. It worked. I heard Nurse Dander gasp and then hurry out of the apartment and down the stairs to see if all the ruckus was the girl she was looking for. I picked up the statue and made sure the blanket was holding tight, and then I hurried down myself. I walked through the abandoned aquarium with my bitten finger in my mouth. "I don't like your cousin," I muttered to all the tadpoles on the counter. In silent tadpole language they said who cares. The floor was still dirty and the door was hanging open, so I didn't have to risk the noise. I stepped out into the street and saw the careful, suspicious figure of Nurse Dander standing by the café, looking this way and that. When she was looking this way, I went that way, and when she was looking that way, I was around the corner.

Ellington was right. It was cold with the sun setting. I wished the blanket were around me instead of the Bombinating Beast. I had it in my hands, and I could have gone anywhere. I could have gone back to the Lost Arms to check in with my chaperone. I could have checked on the Officers Mitchum to see if they had cracked the case. I could have gone back to the library to get Moxie or to Hungry's to see Jake Hix, or walked around until I found Pip and Squeak and had them drive around town looking for Cleo Knight. These are all things you could do, Snicket. I shivered against the side of the building and thought it again. You could do any of these things. You *should* do them. You don't have to meet her. She's a liar and a thief. She's desperate. She's trouble. She stole from you. Nobody knows what you promised. You could keep it to yourself.

But you can tell yourself anything. A wildcat is just one of the wonders of nature, and it's not going to give you nightmares. It was just once on a hike, years ago, and you should forget about it. But then you're sitting up in bed in the middle of the night, heart pounding from the chase, and it doesn't matter what you tell yourself. Your sister is older now. A branch of a tree would no longer hurt her. You don't need to be in the city helping her. You can be here, in Stain'd-by-the-Sea. Nobody is in any danger, I told myself. I clutched the beast to my chest and started walking quickly. You know where, I told myself. Corner of Caravan and Parfait. Black Cat Coffee is where she is waiting.

CHAPTER NINE

If this account can be called a mystery, then Black Cat Coffee is a mystery inside a mystery. There were certainly mysterious things in the establishment. The shiny machinery in the center of the room—which produced bread or coffee, depending on which button you pressed—always worked perfectly, but I never saw anyone attending to it. The attic was a place where you could retrieve packages, but I never saw anyone delivering them. The player piano played tunes I couldn't identify.

But these aren't what I mean. I don't care who oiled the machinery of Black Cat Coffee and made sure the bins were full of flour and roasted beans, or who delivered the boxes of books filled with blank pages or gears used in botanical extraction. The music doesn't matter to me. The real mystery of Black Cat Coffee is the girl with the curved eyebrows and the unreadable smile, who was there at the counter when I arrived, an empty cup and saucer in front of her and another one steaming in front of the neighboring stool. Her hair was still pinned up, but my coat lay folded on the counter.

"I told myself that if you weren't here by the time this coffee cooled," she said, "then you wouldn't be here at all."

"I told you I would meet you," I said.

"You didn't even hide that," she said, and pointed at the Bombinating Beast.

"True," I said, although I kept it tucked underneath my arm.

"Are you going to give it back to me?"

"Are you going to tell me what it is?"

"It's a statue of an imaginary beast."

"It's more than that, and you know it."

"I only know that Hangfire wants it."

"Then why hasn't he gotten it from you?"

Ellington shook her head. "I don't know," she said. "Have a seat, Mr. Snicket. Have some coffee."

She patted the neighboring stool, and I sat down but pushed the coffee away. "You know I'm a teetotaler when it comes to coffee."

"You would like it if you tried it."

"I prefer root beer."

"I've looked all over this town for root beer for you," she said. "I even checked for it yesterday, when I was fooling the woman at Partial Foods. They don't carry it."

"I know," I said. "It's one of the many draw-backs of this town."

She sipped my coffee. "What are the others?"

The disappointments of Stain'd-by-the-Sea seemed too numerous to list. "This town is far from people I would prefer to be closer to," I said, "and it's in the shadow of the treachery of a terrible villain."

"I suppose that's what brought us both here," she said.

"No," I said. "I'm here because my chaper-one is here."

"But why is she here?"

"It's complicated," I said. "It's like a story so long that you end up getting lost in it. Do you know that one about the big fight over an apple and a pretty woman?"

"The one that ends with a hollow statue and a ghost who likes to bury things? My father was reading me that when he disappeared." She finished the coffee and turned the cup upside down on the saucer. It was a nice gesture to watch. "Every night, my father would get home from his fieldwork and leave his boots on the porch. It was during the floods, and his boots got so muddy there was no use washing them. He'd cook dinner in his socks, and then I'd do the dishes, and he'd pour himself a glass of wine and read me a chapter of something before we put the lights out."

"It sounds like a cozy life," I said.

"It was." Ellington's voice was far away, and I could scarcely hear her over the sounds of the player piano. "My father is a naturalist, so our house was always filled with wildflowers from nearby meadows, or baby animals he had rescued, recuperating in old shoe boxes until they were healthy enough to be set free. And he was a lover of music, so he would wind up the record player first thing in the morning so we'd have music with our breakfast. Then one night I didn't hear his boots on the porch, and now that music is all I have."

I thought of the record player, still playing music in that shabby apartment. "I'm sorry you had to leave that behind," I said, "but you might be able to get it back."

"I still have this." Ellington reached into her pocket and laid a small object between the two coffee cups. It looked like the old-fashioned record player, except it was the size of a deck of cards. She wound the tiny crank, and we both leaned forward to hear the little, tinkly music. "My father always carried this music box," she said, "so he could have music with him no matter how far into the wilderness he went. He left it behind on the day he disappeared, so I've been taking care of it."

"I recognize the tune," I said, remembering the first night Ellington and I met. The same music had been playing out of the record player at Handkerchief Heights. It was a tune that was sad but not weepy, as if it were trying to say there was no point in bursting into tears when there was so much work to be done. "What's it called?"

Ellington just shook her head. There are some secrets you want to keep to yourself, even if they don't matter. They might only matter if you keep them secret.

"I saw the rescued tadpole," I said, "in the bowl on the bathroom sink. Do you think your father was there?"

"I don't know. But rescuing a little animal like that is definitely something he would do."

"It might be little, but it's fierce." I held up my finger and showed her the tiny scab where I had been bitten.

"That looks like it hurts."

"It hurts as much as it looks."

"If my father were here, he could fix that," Ellington said. "He would pluck the right herbs growing from cracks in the sidewalk and concoct something that would work in no time. He's a brilliant scientist."

"Stain'd-by-the-Sea needs brilliant scientists," I said. "Perhaps soon your father and Cleo Knight will be working side by side to stop this town from disappearing completely."

"In the meantime," Ellington said with a sigh, "we're alone. We're alone and it's difficult. Don't you find it difficult to be alone, Mr. Snicket?"

I put down the bundle I was holding, the mysterious statue covered in a blanket. "I don't know," I said. "I was taught not to mind."

"Who would teach you a thing like that? S. Theodora Markson?"

"No, no, I learned it long before she became my chaperone."

"Oh yes," she said. "You told me you had an unusual education, but you didn't tell me the details."

"I don't like thinking about the details."

"Digging a tunnel, you told me once. Digging a tunnel to the basement of a museum."

"That's right."

"There are no more museums in Stain'd-by-the-Sea."

"No," I said. "There aren't."

"So you're not doing the digging. Someone else is."

"Yes."

"Someone you would prefer to be closer to, like you said."

"Yes."

"So I guess you mind being alone after all."

"I told you, they taught us not to mind," I said. "They can teach you anything. That doesn't mean you learn it. It doesn't mean you believe it."

"Then can't you go and help whoever is digging that tunnel?"

"No," I said. "I need to stay here."

"Why? Because of Theodora?"

"Because of you," I said. "I promised to help you. Don't you remember, Ms. Feint?"

Ellington looked at me, and her green eyes filled with water. "Yes," she said. "Mr. Snicket, my father is such a gentle man. He must be very frightened, wherever he is. How can we find him?"

"If we find Cleo Knight," I said, "I think we'll find your father. Cleo is a brilliant chemist, and your father is a brilliant naturalist. Hangfire is collecting brilliant people and forcing them to do terrible things."

"My father would never do anything terrible."

I did not answer. I did not know the man. It seemed to me that every adult did something terrible sooner or later. And every child, I thought, sooner or later becomes an adult. I did not like to think this, so I listened instead to the sounds of the player piano tangling with the sounds of Armstrong Feint's music box. I listened until a new sound joined in, a sound I was sad to recognize. It was the sound of a boy about my age, leaning out the window of a station wagon pretending to be a siren. In moments the Officers Mitchum were striding into Black Cat Coffee, followed by their sneering son and a great heap of wild yarn. I had to blink three times before realizing that the yarn was actually S. Theodora Markson, with her hair looking even crazier than it normally did.

"Snicket!" she cried. "There you are!"

"S!" I couldn't resist answering. "Here I am."

"These officers were looking for you, Snicket. They interrupted me in the middle of a shampoo. I told them that you like to waste your days here, mooning over your cupidity for Elaine."

"Her name is Ellington Feint," I said, "and she is sitting right here."

"We're not interested in where your friends are sitting," Harvey Mitchum told me. "We're interested in what you're up to."

"My chaperone told me to make myself scarce until dinnertime," I said.

"Did she also tell you to send the police on a wild-goose chase?" demanded Mimi Mitchum. "You wasted the time of the law, and of the law's son, who could have been doing something more constructive with his time."

"It's true," Stew said to me with a phoniness the adults had no ear to catch. "I was going to give myself a spelling test, but instead you wasted my afternoon."

It was useless to argue that Stew Mitchum was more likely going to continue his antics with his slingshot, which was sticking prominently out of his pocket.

"You told us to go see the Knight family," Harvey Mitchum said. "You told us silly things about Dr. Flammarion. But instead—"

"Let me tell it, Harvey," Mimi said. "I'm better at telling stories."

"You are not!"

"I am so! Remember that time I told a story at that tea party that our friends' mother held at that restaurant that used to be on the corner near the dry cleaner's where that man used to—"

"You see?" Harvey Mitchum crowed in triumph. "That story is boring already, and you haven't even told it!"

"If I haven't told it, how could it be boring?"

"You could make anything boring, Mimi! You're like a magic wand of boring!"

"Well, you're like a magic wand of bad breath!"

"I get bad breath because I eat what you cook!"

"That's right! You never do the cooking!"

Ellington Feint hadn't spent much time with the Officers Mitchum, but she instinctively knew that the only way to stop them from arguing was to interrupt. "Excuse me," she said, "but what happened when you went to see the Knights?"

Harvey Mitchum gave her an irritated frown. "Nothing happened," he said. "The Knights have left Stain'd-by-the-Sea. The entire Ink Inc. building is boarded up, like almost every other building in town."

I thought of what Zada and Zora had said. What could they do, if Mr. and Mrs. Knight gave the word to leave? They were only the servants. "Are the housekeepers gone?"

"Everyone's gone. You led us to an empty building, Snicket, and we went to your chaperone to find out why."

"I'll tell you why," I said. "Because I'm trying to solve the Cleo Knight case."

"There is no Cleo Knight case," Theodora said firmly. "As I told the officers, no crime has been committed. We know that the Knight girl ran away to join the circus, and we know that her parents moved out of the city."

"We know no such thing," I said. I turned to the officers. "Did you find Dr. Flammarion? Did you talk to him?"

Mimi Mitchum shook her head at me in that way that no one likes to have a head shaken at them. "In the first place," she said, "Dr. Flammarion is a respected apothecary. And in the second place, well, there's not really a second place. The case is closed."

"But Miss Knight's car is still parked in front of Partial Foods."

"Be sensible, Snicket. Miss Knight was seen leaving Partial Foods and getting into a cab."

"That wasn't Miss Knight," Ellington said calmly. "That was me."

"You?" Harvey Mitchum said sternly.

"Yes. I was playing a trick on that grocer."

"So you and the Snicket lad were fooling us together?"

"Mr. Snicket knew nothing of this," Ellington said, "until he ran into me here."

I once had a pair of pants that fit me like Ellington's story fit the truth. They fell down as soon as I took a few steps.

"Then I'm afraid you're under arrest," Mimi Mitchum said sternly, and grabbed Ellington's arm. "Playing tricks is called fraud, and fraud is a crime."

"This isn't right," I said. "You should be looking for Miss Knight, not arresting Ms. Feint."

"Don't tell us our business," Harvey Mitchum said sternly. "This girl was involved in robbery not long ago, and now is guilty of fraud. It's still too early to make assumptions, but it wouldn't be surprising if she were involved in all of the other suspicious shenanigans around town."

"Like those threats to the library," Mimi said.

"Or those stolen melons," her husband said.

"Or the broken glass in that alley."

Harvey Mitchum looked Ellington Feint straight in her green eyes. "You're in a great deal of trouble, young lady. You'll likely be on the next train to the city, where you will be imprisoned for your crimes. In the meantime, we'll take you down to the station and lock you up until all of us know what's what."

I did not like to think about how long it would take for all of us to know what was what. My own chaperone did not yet know how to acceptably style her hair, and she'd been growing it for years. The Officers Mitchum marched Ellington out the door, and I put on my coat and tucked the Bombinating Beast under my arm before following them.

"What a beautiful blankie," Stewart cooed to me, pointing at the light blue fringe.

"I'm glad you like it," I told him, "but it's not for sale."

"It's too bad you don't want to do business with me," he said, giving me a very dark look. "I'm going to be very important around here."

"You already are," I said. "You're the sweetest boy the town's ever seen."

"Keep joking," Stew said. "You just keep on joking and see where it gets you."

"I guess I should be scared," I said. "You're good with a slingshot."

The officers' son leaned in close. "And I have a friend," he murmured, "who is good with a knife."

I blinked at him and saw him in a new light, a phrase which here means that I no longer thought he was harmless. We are all told to ignore bullies. It's something they teach you, and they can teach you anything. It doesn't mean you learn it. It doesn't mean you believe it. One should never ignore bullies. One should stop them.

"Hop in, Snicket," Harvey Mitchum said, hopping in himself. It was apparently his turn to drive. "We'll give you and your chaperone a ride as far as the station."

"Very kind of you," Theodora said. "I'm sorry my youngster was so much trouble."

The adults piled into the front of the car, and the children got into the back, which is the way of the world. Stew leaned his head out of the window and started sirening, and Ellington looked straight ahead and did not say anything to me. I let her think things through and listened to the adults. The difficulty of caring for children, they said. Disobedience, they said. Authority. A difficult age. When they were children, they never would have dared to do what children do nowadays without batting an eye. If their grandparents were alive to see this, they would roll in their graves. I began to listen to the sputter of the station wagon instead. It made more sense.

The Mitchums parked, and we walked across the lawn, past the statue that had melted in the explosion. We walked up the steps and into the station. The station looked even less impressive than it had that morning. Maybe it was because that morning I'd thought the police might do the right thing. They led Ellington Feint to the far end of the room and put her in the cell. I watched her sit down on the cot, and Stew took this opportunity to kick me in the calf while nobody else was looking. He kicked hard. I wished I had the biting tadpole handy. The adults were still shaking their heads over the sad state of today's youth, so I went to Ellington and looked over her situation.

"It's an ordinary enough pin tumbler lock," I said to her in a quiet murmur. "You can do it with one of your hairpins. Think of the lock as containing a tiny chest of drawers. If you open all of the drawers the exact right amount, the lock will open."

She gave me a tiny nod. "I won't be able to do it," she murmured back, "unless you lure them away."

"The police are on to my tricks," I said, "but I'll try to give them a real reason to leave the station. In the meantime, at least you're safe."

"Anything is safe," she said, "if it's locked in here."

I stepped back, just slightly. Ellington stood up from the cot.

"Give it to me," she said. "It's the best place for it."

"Come along now, Snicket," Theodora called to me. "We've been in these officers' hair long enough."

It was impossible not to smile when Theodora said the word "hair." Ellington smiled too. "She'll ask you what it is," she said.

"She won't notice," I said.

"She'll notice."

"Well, then I'll tell her."

"You won't tell her."

But Theodora had reached me. "What's that?" she said, frowning at what I was holding. I looked at Ellington Feint. Ellington Feint watched me.

"It's my security blanket," I said.

"Security blanket?" Theodora repeated with a frown. "Be sensible, Snicket. It's not proper for someone of your age to have a security blanket. Give it to me."

"I thought I would give it to Ms. Feint," I said, "in case she found it difficult to be alone."

"I'm teaching myself not to mind," Ellington said quietly.

"They can teach you anything," I said, and took the statue from underneath my arm. Even covered by a childish blanket, it felt dark, and mysterious, and even menacing. I felt its weight in my hands as I passed it through the bars. They can teach you anything. It doesn't mean you learn it. It doesn't mean you believe it. I couldn't believe it myself, that I was giving Ellington Feint the Bombinating Beast.

CHAPTER TEN

Moxie was waiting for me right outside the police station. She looked cross. She'd even put down her typewriter, right by the door of the library, so she could cross her arms. She did it crossly.

"Don't be mad, Moxie."

"I *am* mad," she said. "I sat in the library reading about military history for hours, and when I went to show you what I'd found, you'd snuck out."

Theodora put a stern hand on my shoulder. "'Snuck' is not proper," she said to Moxie. "The correct term is 'sneaked.' And it does not surprise me that Snicket has disappointed you, whoever you are."

Moxie turned her eyes from me to my chaperone and then reached into the brim of her hat. "I'm Moxie Mallahan," she said, handing Theodora one of her printed cards. "*The News.* We've met before."

"I'm not interested in discussing imaginary meetings," Theodora said, absently tucking Moxie's card into her hair. "I've had a very trying day. I solved a case in a few minutes, but then my apprentice spent the afternoon sending the police on a wild-goose chase. His little friend has been arrested, and I'm considering putting him back on probation."

Recently I'd figured out the difference between being on probation and not being on probation. The difference was that if I were on probation, Theodora could remind me I was on probation, and if I were not on probation, Theodora could remind me that she could put me back on probation. Theodora snuck a look at me to see what I thought of what she'd said. I looked at the ground.

"I'm sorry to hear that, Ms. Markson," Moxie said, trying not to stare at Theodora's hair. "A person of your great skill shouldn't have to be bothered by inept apprentices. If you solved a case today, you should be celebrating, not disciplining troublesome underlings."

Theodora's voice softened slightly, like an old onion. "I quite agree," she said. "Perhaps you're more sensible than I first thought."

"That's very sweet of you to say," Moxie said politely.

"Snicket, make yourself scarce," Theodora said. "I'm going to celebrate the solving of this case."

"I'll look after him, Ms. Markson," Moxie

said. "That way he'll be out of your…"

I watched Moxie's face as she did something very difficult. A laugh is harder to swallow whole than a honeydew melon. Her mouth twisted every which way, and her eyes flitted madly as she looked everywhere but at me. "Out of your hair, Ms. Markson," she finished finally. "Out of your hair."

Theodora gave Moxie a nod and strode down the stairs. We waited until it was safe to open up the laugh, and then we shared it. "You have a very good polite voice," I told her.

"That's very sweet of you to say," she said again. "My mother said a good polite voice is the journalist's best tool because people are more likely to tell you important information if you treat them nicely. She had an expression for it—you catch more flies with honey than with vinegar."

"Either way," I said, "you end up with flies.

Did your mother teach you the phrase 'trouble-some underlings'?"

"My father used to call everyone at the news-paper that, as a joke." She stared out at the lawn, the damaged statue, and the darkening sky. "Back when the newspaper was running," she said, "and when my father was in a jokey mood."

"It's a good phrase," I said.

"You might not be a troublesome underling, Snicket, but you are still troublesome. You said we were associates, and then you ran out of the library without telling me."

"I had to follow someone."

"I would have gone with you."

"I keep telling you, Moxie, I don't want to lead you into danger."

She reached down and picked up her type-writer. "I'm a journalist, Snicket. A dangerous story is an interesting story, and interesting stories belong in the newspaper. Now tell me everything that happened since you sneaked out of the library—"

"*Snuck*," I said, but Moxie just shook her head.

"When did you leave? Who did you follow? How did you know to follow them? Where did they go? What did you find? Why aren't you telling me?"

I sat down on the steps. "I'll tell you," I said.

She opened her typewriter. "Everything," she reminded me.

I told her everything. She typed wildly, like she was hurrying after something. She took off her hat and scratched her forehead in thought. "So Ellington Feint pretended to be Cleo Knight, so Cleo could stay in town and finish her formula for invisible ink."

"But Ms. Feint took her Cleo Knight act to the Inhumane Society to get closer to Hangfire and rescue her father."

"And meanwhile Cleo was kidnapped, and nobody's seen or heard from her."

"Maybe somebody has," I said suddenly. "Are you hungry?"

"Yes, I am."

"That's funny. I thought somebody else was Hungry."

"I don't follow you, Snicket."

"Then follow me, Moxie."

Moxie followed me. The last few rays of sun lit the lawn in dim stripes. The shape of the ruined statue made a long, strange shadow. "You haven't even asked me what *I* discovered," Moxie said.

"I thought you were too mad to tell me."

She frowned at me. "I didn't appreciate being left at the library, but I did find some interesting information. Dashiell Qwerty stopped by to check on me, and he just happened to leave a book on the table that turned out to be important. Isn't that a strange coincidence?"

"It might be serendipity," I said, "or it might be something else."

"Whenever I talk with you, I get the feeling there's *something else*," Moxie said to me. "You're chasing mysteries, Snicket, but you've been a mystery yourself since you arrived in town. I have the sense there's something you're not telling me—something secret underneath the surface, like an underground tunnel."

I froze. "What exactly did you find out?"

Moxie walked over to the remains of the statue and ran her hands down the cold, melted metal. "Remember that photograph I showed you?"

I nodded. "It was the groundbreaking ceremony, with everyone gathered to celebrate the first day of work on the statue honoring Colonel Colophon."

"Not everyone was celebrating," Moxie said. "The book Qwerty left on the table talked about what happened beforehand. There was a fierce argument over the statue, and after the groundbreaking ceremony the argument only got fiercer.

There were people who thought that the war was nothing to celebrate and that Colonel Colophon shouldn't be honored for so much bloodshed. The tree that was uprooted was home to the Farnsworth Pulpeater Moths, and people were angry that no one had thought of what would happen to those rare and endangered creatures. At first there were only a few people who thought this way, and they began to make trouble. They even formed a sort of troublemaking society."

"The Inhumane Society," I said.

Moxie blinked at me. "I knew it," she said. "I knew you'd know."

"I didn't know, really," I said. "I guessed."

"You're a good guesser."

"I have good associates."

We'd reached the door of Hungry's, and I held it open for Moxie, who sat immediately at the counter and typed a few lines. Pip and Squeak looked up at the sound and gave us a wave, and

199

Jake Hix gave us a salute from the stove, where he was standing over something sizzling with a spatula in his hand.

"Did you finish that mystery?" I asked him.

"Not quite," Jake said.

"Well, maybe you can help me with mine."

Jake slid the sizzles onto two plates and then hovered over them with a pepper grinder. "Let me just serve this up, and I'll come talk to you," he said.

"What are you fixing?"

"Gashouse eggs. Let me whip some up for you."

"Me too, Jake," said Moxie, without looking up from her notes.

Jake gave her a smile and delivered dinner to the Bellerophon brothers. "Sure thing, Moxie. Haven't seen you around for a while. How've you been?"

"Busy," Moxie said, and kept typing while Jake got to work tossing another cube of butter

into a hot, flat pan. "Tell me," I said to Pip, "why didn't you mention that you picked up Ellington Feint in your cab the other day?"

"You didn't ask," Pip said, with his mouth full.

"You just asked about Cleo Knight," Squeak said.

Jake frowned into the butter. "If that's what this is about, maybe I don't want to talk to you after all, Snicket," he told me. "I said before, I don't talk about my customers."

"You're good at keeping secrets," I said, "but you could be better. You slipped up. You said you didn't know her very well, and then you called her Cleo. Everybody calls her Miss Knight. Even her parents call her Miss Knight. You must be pretty close friends if you're calling her Cleo."

Jake was silent for a minute. He sliced two big hunks of bread and ripped a hole in each of them, right in the middle, and then slid the two hunks into the sizzling pan along with a handful of spinach and a few mushrooms. He got two eggs ready to crack, and he still didn't look at me. Gashouse eggs are sunny-side-up eggs cooked in the middle of a piece of bread. It's like French toast and fried eggs are dancing together, with some spinach and mushrooms playing the tune. He was sore at me, but he was still cooking me dinner. Jake Hix was a person of honor.

"We're not friends," he said, finally and quietly. "We're sweethearts, OK? Go ahead and laugh if you want to."

"I never laugh at a man's romantic life," I said. "That's his own business."

"Well, the Knight family doesn't feel that way," he said. "They don't think it's proper to have a hash slinger like me involved with their brilliant chemist."

"A chemist and a cook are basically doing the same thing," I said. "It all comes down to mixing and heating some basic elements."

Pip pointed to his meal with his fork. "Then I'd call you a brilliant chemist, Hix."

Jake smiled and covered the pan. "Well, Mr. and Mrs. Knight put up such a fuss that Cleo and I had to keep things secret. But now that the Knights have left town, there's no reason to keep sneaking around."

"Does that mean this is on the record?" Moxie asked, her fingers poised over the typewriter keys.

"Sure," Jake said. He wiped his hands on a towel and slung it over his shoulder. "Cleo is hiding out, working on a big experiment. When she's done, Stain'd-by-the-Sea will be a real town again, and Cleo and I will get married."

"I'm afraid that's not the case," I said.

"Sure it is," Jake said. "Cleo made a deal with some girl. They dyed her hair and dressed her up in the same clothes so that anyone who went looking for her would be on the wrong track.

Sorry, Snicket, but you've been barking up the wrong tree."

"I barked up that tree and found a bird anyway," I said. "Listen, Jake. Has Cleo called you?"

Jake shook his head. "She said it might be a little while," he said. "I'm not nervous about it, though. Cleo's not afraid of anything except heights and not finishing her formula."

I looked at him and asked him the question on the cover of this book.

"Yesterday morning, right outside this diner," Jake said, pointing with a spatula. He uncovered the pan, and the steam rose into his face. "She had tea here, and then she got into her Dilemma and drove off. It's like I told you before, Snicket. I just didn't tell you all of it."

He served up the gashouse eggs, first to Moxie and then to me. I knew they'd be delicious, but I didn't want to eat them. I didn't want to be at Hungry's telling Jake Hix the bad news.

"Cleo Knight's Dilemma is parked a block away with a flat tire," I said. "The family apothecary grabbed her, Hix."

Jake Hix went white. "No," he said. "Now you're not telling me the truth, Snicket."

"I'm afraid so," I said. "I think she's in the clutches of a doctor named Flammarion and a villain named Hangfire. She should be at the Colophon Clinic." I looked down the counter at Pip and Squeak. "I'd appreciate a ride," I said, "so we can get her back."

"Of course," Pip said. "Let's go."

Everyone got up from the counter, and Jake Hix tossed the towel down to the ground and turned a sign around in the window so it read CLOSED. "Why didn't you tell me before, Snicket?" he asked. "Why'd you let me chatter away when all the while my sweetheart was in danger?"

"I'm sorry," I said. "I had to be sure."

"Sure of what?"

"Sure I could trust you," I said. "You lied to me before."

"Of course you can trust me," Jake Hix said. "We read the same books."

"Will there be room for everybody in the cab?" Moxie asked, snapping shut the typewriter case.

"If we squeeze," Squeak squeaked.

Jake shook his head. "I'll take the Dilemma," he said. "It'll only take me a second to change the tire. I'll meet you all at the Colophon Clinic."

"You'll find two melons under the car," I said. "I'd be grateful if you'd return them to Partial Foods."

Jake was so worried he didn't ask me why. In a second we were outside and he was sprinting around the corner to Cleo's car. It was getting chilly. There was a cranky wind, and here and there I could see white papers blowing hither and yon and then hither again. They looked like dried-up plants that had broken from their roots and let the wind roll them anyplace. I'd seen them once on a trip to the mountains with my parents. Tumbleweeds. But these were the posters for Cleo Knight's disappearance, blowing away. MISSING. If we don't find her soon, I thought, she'll be gone forever.

Moxie turned to me as we got into the taxi. "Are you sure you can trust *me*, Snicket?"

"Sure I'm sure," I said, "and that goes for you two up front as well."

"Much obliged," Squeak said. He meant "thank you," and his brother said it in the regular way.

"If you trust me," Moxie said, "why do I have the feeling there are things you're not telling me?"

"There are things you're not telling me, too," I said. "There are things everyone isn't telling everybody."

That ended the chitchat. The taxi rattled its way through the streets and then along a long,

straight road out of town. I kept my eyes forward. Nobody spoke. The Bellerophon brothers
didn't even ask for a tip. Had they asked, I would
have told them about a book I was thinking about
on the drive. It was a book about a girl named
Kit who acquires a reputation for witchcraft. It
gets her into a lot of trouble, but she does manage to find someone she can trust. His name is
Nathaniel, and he names a ship after her. The
ship is called *The Witch*, but I couldn't remember the name of the author. I also didn't want
to think about who liked this book more than
I did, someone whose name was also Kit. She
and I had something in common about now. We
were both heading for the wrong place, an enormous, dark place that looked like it was going
to swallow us up. In my case it was tall, iron
gates, much taller and fiercer than gates usually
need to be. On one gate it said COLOPHON, and
the other said CLINIC. The gates were already
open, wide open, like a hug from someone you

don't like. We went in through the gates. It was night now, and the gates closed behind us with a deep *clang* as soon as we drove through, like they weren't tall and fierce to keep people out, but tall and fierce to keep people in.

The Bellerophon brothers stopped the cab. It was dead quiet. In my sister's case it was probably worse, I told myself, but do you think she's as scared as you are? What do you think, Snicket? Do you think you can be as brave as she is? I didn't feel brave. I stared out at the night, where all my questions might be answered, but the shivers on my spine told me I was nowhere near brave enough.

CHAPTER ELEVEN

The Colophon Clinic didn't have to look wicked to be a wicked place, but it did. It was made of black stone with small, narrow windows cut into it here and there, as if someone had taken a knife to the building. To get to the front door, you had to go up a set of broken stairs growing slick black moss in the cracks. There was a tower stuck into the top, very tall and very thin, and there were sharp-looking shingles all over the roof. I don't know why wicked places generally look wicked. You'd think they'd look nice, to fool people, but they hardly ever do. Even the sky was helping out by looking like it would rain. Even the bushes, even the flowers on the bushes, looked like they wanted to hurt somebody. Pip peered at the place doubtfully through the windshield. "This doesn't look good, Snicket."

"No, it doesn't," I said. "You can let me out here in the driveway. I'll see you back in town."

"Oh, sure, I'll let you out," Pip said. "'See you back in town,' he says. Let you out in front of a place like this and see you back in town. Sure, that's something nice guys like me and my brother would do. Nothing wrong with leaving a guy all alone in a dangerous place. Maybe on our way into town we can find a puppy to run over because we're such nice guys."

"We're staying here, Snicket," Squeak translated, crawling up to sit next to his brother. "The gates closed behind us anyway."

212

"And you know you're stuck with me," Moxie said.

"You look like I could talk you out of that," I said.

She smiled and frowned and shook her head.

"What's going to be in there?" Pip asked.

"I have no idea," I admitted. "Maybe Cleo Knight. Maybe Dr. Flammarion and his needles and Nurse Dander and her knives and maybe the whole Inhumane Society with a trained cackle of vicious hyenas. We won't know until we go in."

"You're not much of a detective, are you?"

"I'm not a detective at all," I said. It was something they told us again and again, over the course of our childhoods, from the day we could understand what the words meant to the day we graduated and were sent out into the world. "It looks like I'm solving mysteries, but I'm not. I'm just poking around. What we do, my associates and I, is like wandering the stacks of a library. We don't really know what we'll find. We just hope it will be helpful."

"That's a strange job," Pip said.

"It's more of an occupation."

"It's a strange occupation, then."

"Admittedly, it's sometimes hard to find volunteers."

"Why would anybody volunteer to do something like that?"

"Why do you drive this cab?"

"You know why, Snicket," Squeak said. "We do it because our father is sick and can't do it himself."

"I do what I do for basically the same reason."

"I don't understand," Moxie said quietly.

I brushed my hands on my pants, like I was getting rid of something stuck to me. "Who else is going to do it?" I said. "Let's get to work. They closed the gates, which means they saw us coming. But they don't know how many of us there are. It would be foolish to walk in all together. Who has a watch?"

"I have my father's," Moxie said, rolling up her sleeve to show me.

"I have my father's, too," Squeak said.

"Moxie and I will go in together," I said. "Wait ten minutes and then walk in yourself. Ask for your money for the trip out here. Be loud and rude about it. OK?"

"OK," Pip said.

"We'd better synchronize our watches," Moxie said, and held her wrist next to Squeak's. They adjusted their watches so the times matched up exactly. "It's precisely three minutes until eight o'clock," she said, "*now*."

"At seven minutes after, expect the Bellerophon brothers," Squeak said.

"Lie low until then," I said, and got out of the car. The rain dropped its first few tries. Moxie and I started toward the steps. I remembered a lesson of mine, and walked over to the bushes and quickly picked a good handful of flowers.

"Do you have a ribbon, Moxie?"

"What?"

"A hair ribbon, a length of string, anything like that?"

"I have my typewriter ribbon," Moxie said, gesturing to her case, "but I can't type without it, and they're very hard to find in town."

"Never mind then," I said. I held the flowers in my hands in a rough bouquet. They might fool somebody and they might not. I was dressed well enough. We walked up the steps. One of my feet slid in a path of slick moss, leaving a muddy smell on my shoe. A drop of rain hit the moss and sizzled. I had not seen rain sizzle on moss. It made me stop.

Moxie took my arm. "Come on," she said. "Remember what you told me back at the Sallis mansion? Get scared later, Snicket."

The doors were heavy and glass, and it took

the two of us to open one of them. Then we were inside a tall room, full of windows doing the best they could to make the room light and airy. They were doing a bad job of it. There were some expensive sofas to sit on, and here and there were the kind of paintings that make people say their five-year-olds could paint them. Gloomy five-year-olds, in this case. In the middle of the room was a large desk towered with papers, and sitting at the desk with her hands folded was Nurse Dander. She looked right at us, and her fingers rippled. I didn't like it. Never in my life have I liked a receptionist.

"Yes?" she said.

"Delivery," I said. "Flowers for a…" I made a big show of looking at a label that wasn't there. "Colonel Colonic?"

"Colonel Colophon," Nurse Dander corrected.

"Colonel Colophon."

"There is no such person at the Colophon Clinic."

"If there's no such person as Colonel Colophon at the Colophon Clinic, how did you know what name I meant?"

"Leave the flowers here and get out. I'll give them to Colophon."

I shook my head. "I'm supposed to give them directly to the colonel."

Nurse Dander flushed. "Don't provoke me," she said. "The police were notified the moment you drove onto our grounds. This is private property."

"Well, these are private flowers."

Moxie put a hand on my shoulder. "I'm so sorry," she said to the nurse, in her best polite voice. "A person of your great skill shouldn't be bothered by troublesome underlings. If you just let my associate deliver these flowers, I promise I'll discipline him severely."

Nurse Dander stood up. She was still wearing

her white coat, and one of her hands slid into a pocket. "I'll take him to the colonel myself," she said, "although I can't say he'll be pleased to have a visitor."

"I'll wait here," Moxie said, and put down her case on the heavy desk, between two large piles of papers. "Take your time. I'm sure I can find something interesting to read."

Nurse Dander took her hand out of her pocket and put it on top of one of the piles of papers. I looked at the top sheet. I recognized it. I recognized it from a small cottage near the sea, when Stain'd-by-the-Sea had a sea, and from a shabby apartment above an abandoned aquarium. They were Ellington Feint's papers, the written record of her search for her father. They were important to Ellington, and now they were in the hands of one of Hangfire's associates. The nurse looked from the papers to me to Moxie. I couldn't help feeling sorry for her, just a little bit. She'd been told to make sure nobody entered the building and to make sure nobody took the papers on the desk. She couldn't do both.

"I'll find my own way," I said. Nurse Dander didn't answer but kept her eyes on Moxie. This is the dangerous part, I wanted to tell her. This is why I didn't want to have you along. But the journalist looked calm. She was opening her typewriter case and paused only to tap her fingers a couple of times on the face of her watch as I walked by the desk and turned a corner to begin my exploration of the clinic. She was right. There probably wasn't much time. I had no watch. Everything my father had given me I had left at a train station some time ago.

One way to mark time, if you have no watch, is to whistle or hum a piece of music you know by heart. If the piece of music is five minutes long, then when it's over, five minutes have passed. Of course, you have to know how long the tune is. I didn't know how long this one was. I didn't even know what it was called. But I knew it by heart, from hearing it on Ellington's old-fashioned record player and from the music box her father had left behind. I liked the tune. It made for good company.

A clinic is very much like a hospital, and something is wrong when a hospital is empty. When I walked past the desk, I found myself in a hallway that looked like a painting of a hall-way. No one was there—no doctors, no patients, nobody visiting anybody sick. There was a clean smell in the air, but it was not pleasant. Somebody had scrubbed at everything, and then the whole place had been painted. An empty wheelchair sat against one of the walls, and a few doors hung gaping open. I didn't hear anything. I looked through the first door and saw a small bed. I didn't like it. It was an ordinary hospi-tal room, but the bed was too small. I could fit in it, but I wouldn't be comfortable. There was nothing else in the room but something metal on the floor. From the doorway it looked like a snake, wound around one of the legs of the bed.

I stepped closer. It was a chain, thick and cold in my hands. One end was attached to the bed and the rest curled on the floor, ending in a curved metal shape. It looked like the letter *O*, hinged so it could open into the letter *C*. I opened it and closed it, opened it and closed it. A device like this is called a shackle. It's an old word, but that doesn't mean that people don't use such contraptions anymore.

"I don't know what I expected," I said, "but I didn't expect this."

The shackle didn't answer me. I started whistling the tune all over again.

The next three rooms were the same story, and it was not a story I liked. *Like an underground tunnel*, Moxie had said, and I thought of my sister, also walking alone in an empty place. The hallway curved this way and that, and all of the rooms looked identical. My shoes dirtied the clean floor a little, marking my path with bits of black moss. Finally I reached a large, open room. The tall windows, running from the ceiling to the rug, told me this was the back of the clinic, and I could see some tall, close trees, swaying a little in the rain and dropping leaves into the swimming pool, with its dark, wooden bench that I recognized from a photograph. At the far end of the room was the beginning of a winding staircase, narrow metal step after narrow metal step leading up to the tower. Cleo Knight was afraid of heights, I remembered. They would keep her in the tower.

If it seems like there's something I'm not saying, something about the room, that's because there is. The room had three very long tables, banked by very long benches. On the tables were long glass rectangles. It took me a few seconds. Then I recognized them. Fish tanks, from the aquarium. And placed at regular intervals were the same chains, with the same heavy shapes and hinges, that I had seen attached to the small beds.

They would chain them to the tables. And they would chain them to the beds. Nobody was here yet, but everything was ready for children to arrive at the Colophon Clinic and be prisoners of the Inhumane Society. The rain beat on the windows, and I walked up the stairs. It was narrower than I'd thought, very narrow. It was like climbing up a drinking straw. My shoes were loud, and my whistling echoed all the way up. I kept whistling. Why not? If there was anyone there, they knew I was coming.

Then there was a voice at the top, calling something. I stopped short.

"Ellington?" It was a man's voice.

"Mr. Feint?" I called. "Armstrong Feint?"

I moved quicker, farther up the stairs. My footsteps clattered. It was true. It wasn't like solving a mystery at all. I wasn't even doing what I was supposed to be doing. I was supposed to be celebrating the end of the case with my chaperone in the Far East Suite. I was supposed to be deep under the city, moving quickly and quietly through a secret tunnel, or perhaps I would already be in the museum with the item in my hands, following my sister to the exit, which was also a secret. I wasn't supposed to be here. Nobody thought Lemony Snicket should be climbing the steps of the Colophon Clinic on the outskirts of Stain'd-by-the-Sea. It was reckless, what I was doing. It was careless. It was dangerous. It was the right thing to do. Nobody should be chained to anything. "Mr. Feint?" I called again. "Armstrong Feint?"

But it was not Armstrong Feint in the room at the top of the stairs. I was wrong again. This room was fancier and brighter. It had none of the clean, empty feel of the rest of the clinic. There was nothing of the scrubbed smell. It was a room I wouldn't mind living in, if I could bring some books. There weren't any, but there was a big brass bed, all aflow with quilts and blankets and a pile of pillows that made me comfortable just looking at them. There was a large window closed up in curtains, and two tables, one on either side of the bed. One was crowded with a small plate with some bread crumbs and a napkin and a candle and a glass of wine and the bottle it came from. The other had nothing on it, which seemed odd. It had probably had something on it once. The rest of the room was a wide brick fireplace making everything orange. It was a nice fire, but the room was still cold. It probably wasn't cold to the man who was standing by the fire, poking at it with a long iron spike. He'd gotten up from a big, elegant chair with a matching ottoman—a little wooden thing, with a round red cushion built into it—where he'd been putting up his feet. He was dressed in a military uniform that looked old but clean. It was dark gray, and over his heart was a row of medals and honors in different shapes and colors. But instead of shoes he was wearing a pair of curvy slippers, and everywhere his skin should have been—his face, his neck, his hands—there were bandages, wound round and round him like a mummy.

"Colonel Colophon," I said.

The colonel gave me a stiff nod and sat down in his chair. His posture was bad, probably from his injuries. He moved the ottoman away from him and gestured for me to sit down. "I thought you were somebody else," he said, in a faint, hoarse voice made even fainter through the slit in the bandages. "I don't often get visitors."

"I'm here to deliver these flowers," I said. It was strange that I turned out to be doing what I had said I was doing. I'd lied, and now it was true.

The colonel took the flowers in one of his

bandaged hands. "But that's not the only reason you're here," he said. "I know the look of a young man who has a question on his mind."

"The question on my mind," I said, "is whether or not you've seen a young woman. Her name is Cleo Knight, and she's a brilliant chemist."

"As you probably know," the colonel said, "the man who runs this clinic has been trying for a very long time to restore me to health. He's employed all sorts of scientists to help him over the years."

"It doesn't look like Dr. Flammarion is doing much of that lately," I said. "This clinic is entirely empty."

His bandaged head gave a slow nod. "This clinic used to be a bustling place," he said, "but now I'm the only patient left and Dr. Flammarion had to take a job as someone's private apothecary."

"He is working for the Knight family," I said.

"It's their daughter Cleo who has disappeared, and I came looking for her."

"I see. Have I been helpful to you at all?"

"You've been very helpful, Colonel. A number of things that had looked sinister now have very simple explanations. But you still haven't answered my question, Colonel Colophon. Was Cleo Knight here?"

He looked at me and then at the fire, and a cold breeze seemed to rustle through the room. "Yes," he said finally. "She would come here from time to time to study chemistry with Dr. Flammarion. Sometimes she would help as he tried a new treatment on my burns."

I asked the question one last time, the one on the cover of this book.

"Just yesterday," the colonel replied. "She'd had a flat tire, and Dr. Flammarion drove her out here to say good-bye to me. She told me she was tired of chemistry and was running away to join the circus. You see, lad? There's nothing sinister going on at all. It's just that people are moving out of town. Stain'd-by-the-Sea is fading, and its problems are fading along with it. There's nothing here to concern yourself with."

I nodded. "That's a good story," I said. "It answers all of the questions I asked you. But I guess I was asking the wrong questions, wasn't I?"

The slit in the bandages frowned. "What do you mean?"

"I mean, I should have asked you why you called the name you did, when I was coming up the stairs whistling that tune."

"What name?"

"You know what name."

"You must have misheard me, lad."

"You heard the tune," I said, "and you thought you knew who was whistling it. You were afraid that a certain girl had found you at last. You were afraid that she was bringing you the item you asked her to steal, and you'd have to let her father go free."

"I don't know what you're talking about."

"But you don't want to let Armstrong Feint go free," I said, "or Cleo Knight. You and your society aren't done with them. You have a wicked plan."

The man tossed the flowers into the fire. "How dare you call me wicked?" he snarled hoarsely. "I'm a war hero."

"You almost had me thinking you were," I said. "Colonel Colophon is a teetotaler. You should have hidden that glass of wine, Hangfire."

Now his voice changed, now that I'd told him who he was. This voice, if it was his real voice, was much, much worse. "'Teetotaler' is a very fancy word for a little boy to use. Let's test your vocabulary a little more, shall we? Do you know the word 'defenestration'?"

With a flourish he drew back the heavy

curtains, and the wind rushed in. The window had been broken—not shattered, but there was a big, jagged hole in the middle of the pane, roughly the shape of a man. "Defenestration" is a word which means throwing someone out a window. It had clearly happened recently. Hangfire hooked his bandaged fingers around my neck and dragged me to peer out through the jagged hole at the rain and the trees and the dark waters of the swimming pool, where the real Colonel Colophon had fallen. The waters were troubled, churning in the rain like a storm at sea.

"Listen," he hissed in my ear. "Listen carefully, Snicket."

Through the sound of rain and the wind in the trees, I heard another sound. It was a sort of rumbling, or a sort of hum. Hangfire pushed me closer to the window, and I struggled against him. It was a tense dance. My mossy foot slipped on the carpet, and when my hands grabbed at

his coat, one of his medals poked my finger right where the tadpole had bitten me. The sound grew louder.

"Do you hear it?" he hissed.

"Dilemma," I managed to say.

"Don't be ridiculous," he said. "It's no dilemma for me to destroy you, Snicket."

"That's not the sort of Dilemma I mean," I said, and his eyes widened beneath his bandages. A dilemma can refer to a difficult choice, of course, but the sound I had heard, over the rain and the wind, was the engine of a fancy automobile, the sort that can crash through a wall and emerge without a dent or a scratch, although the building might collapse. I had heard this many times but had never seen it tested until tonight. The Dilemma emerged through the trees, skidded around the swimming pool, and crashed into the back of the Colophon Clinic. It was something to see. Like all big accidents, it looked wrong somehow, as if it were impossible that it had actually happened. But it had happened. It rattled the roof. It shook the entire building. It sent a large crack down the wall, with a noise like someone's leg breaking. It knocked the villain to the floor.

I stood up, freed from Hangfire's grasp. There he is, I thought, and here you are. The villain got to his feet and backed away from me, toward the broken and chilly window. One of his hands reached up to his face, and he unpeeled one of the bandages slightly. I didn't like looking at it. Then Hangfire stood on his tiptoes and reached up over his head. He stuck the edge of the bandage on a jagged edge of broken glass, like he was hanging a hat on a hook. Then he spread his arms out wide and took a step back from me, and another.

In three steps he was out the window. The bandage unraveled as he fell, and when I leaned out, I saw him grasping the unfurling bandage and dragging his feet against the cracked outside wall of the clinic, slowing and softening his fall. The building kept shaking and kept creaking. It was too dark to see his face, of course. Like all villains, he was a coward and would not face me unmasked. I saw the dim figure of Hangfire let go of the bandage and jump the rest of the way, landing at the edge of the swimming pool. The bandage made a little rustle as it unwrapped—the sound a spider might make when it spun a web, if you got close enough to hear it. The water splashed, like one of his shoes had fallen in, or perhaps something had splashed out of the water. I couldn't see. He paused for a moment and ran nimbly into the trees. There he goes, I thought, and here you are. You are out of his clutches. Now you've got to rescue everyone else.

CHAPTER TWELVE

No one was after me, but I still ran all the way down the stairs. The sound of the rain grew louder as I hurried, until at last I was in the room with all of the wooden tables. The tables were still there. The benches were still there, and the fish tanks, and the shackles. But where the window had been was now a wonder of an automobile, shiny with raindrops, having come to a stop in a pile of broken glass. They were right, the manufacturers of the Dilemma. Not a dent, not a scratch. But Jake Hix, unhooking his seat belt and opening the door of the car, looked as shaken as the building.

"Where's my sweetheart?" he asked me, shouting over the rain.

"Some people park their cars," I said, "and walk through the door."

"The door was locked," Jake said. "I could see people moving around inside, but nobody would let me in. There was a taxi parked out front, but there was nobody in it. Where is she, Snicket?"

Something in the building groaned, the groan of metal and bricks that are beginning to give up. "I can't find her, but she's here somewhere."

"How do you know?"

"Hangfire was very eager for me to think there was nothing here to concern myself with."

"Who's Hangfire?"

"Just think of someone rotten, Jake. I'll explain later."

For a moment I thought that Jake Hix had thought of someone so rotten that it made him scream. But Jake's mouth was closed and worried. The screams were from someplace else, muffled but frantic, with some thumpings along with them. He and I looked at each other and looked around, but it was hard to tell, over the rain, where the screams were coming from.

It is awful. It is a wretched feeling to know that someone needs help and you are not helping. I had already asked it once in Stain'd-by-the-Sea, the question "Where is that screaming coming from?" and although it had not been the wrong question, the answer was still terrible.

I ran over to the bottom of the spiral staircase and peered back up at where I had been. The screams weren't coming from there. Jake stepped carefully through the broken window and scanned the rain and the trees and the rippling pool. I shook my head to him and he shook his head to me, and we walked toward each other until we were in the middle of the room. Somehow the screams were louder. But the room is empty, I thought to myself. Think, Snicket. Jake Hix works at a diner, but you've been taught what to do in these situations. I looked above me but saw only the rafters of the room. I leaned down to look under the tables, although Hangfire couldn't hide a screaming girl unnoticed under a table any more than my sister could hide her diary unnoticed under her pillow. Nevertheless, the screams were louder when I looked. I knelt down on the rug, and they were louder still. The rug I hadn't looked at much. It was blood red, with small black swirls patterned in a row. The swirls, I saw, were little sea horses with sharp teeth and vicious eyes. Even on a rug the Bombinating Beast was something horrible.

I stood up and pushed at one of the tables. "Help me move this," I said, and Jake understood immediately. The screams continued, along with a few thumps, as we pushed a table as far as we could, knocking over benches. We moved those too. The rug was very large, and we had to move all the furniture to the walls, quickly. Fish tanks shattered to the ground. We didn't care what happened to anything. I'd never done something like that and, even under the circumstances, it was a little fun. I understood bullies better. I understood why you'd want to push things around without caring if you caused any damage.

The screams were quite clear now. *Help!* is what the screams were saying.

"Hang on, Cleo!" Jake called, with his hands cupped to his mouth. We kicked a few more benches into a corner, and then the rug was clear, and Jake and I rolled it up together. The rug was thick and didn't want to be rolled up.

We rolled it up. Then there was only the wooden floor, pale and dusty, with a large hatch in the middle of it. It was metal, with a circle of bolts along the edges and a big dark ring you could pull to open it. Over the ring there were two initials etched into the metal. It takes a long time to etch letters into metal, and it made me furious. The reason it made me furious was that I knew my sister was probably standing in front of a hatch with etched initials, perhaps at the very same moment. They were different initials, but there in the rainy room, with the screams and thumps below us, it didn't matter. It felt the same. Adults etching initials into a hatch and then shutting a hatch so nobody could reach the important secrets, the noble people, the secret formula that might save the town. The hatch was the problem, the hatch with the initials I.S. etched into it, for "Inhumane Society," and I was going to get it open.

I knelt down and tugged, and Jake knelt down

and tugged with me. The ring was big enough for both of our hands, and then all four of our hands, tugging together. It was like tugging on the world. It did not move. "Cleo!" Jake shouted every so often, and the screams continued. *Help! Help! Someone help me!* I did not shout anything. I was afraid I would shout my sister's name. We tugged and tugged, and finally Jake Hix looked at me.

"It's not budging."

"I know it's not budging," I said. "We need to pull harder."

"Maybe it opens from the inside."

"No, the handle is here."

Jake looked at me and rubbed his eyes a little bit. "But how do you know it's possible, Snicket? How do you know we can do it?"

"Hangfire did it," I said. "We need to open this hatch, Jake. We need to open it now."

"My aunt always says that if you put your mind to it, you can do absolutely anything," Jake said. "Is that true?"

"No," I said. "It's nonsense. But we can open this hatch. Come on now, Hix. On the count of three."

It is never seven that you count to, before you do something difficult. It is never at the count of two. It is always three, and it is strange. One, two, three, and then Jake and I pulled on the ring very hard. Our hands strained together at the task, and our faces had terrible frowns. We probably looked ridiculous, and we probably sounded ridiculous. But ridiculous or not, we were going to open the hatch. It doesn't matter if you look ridiculous, not if you are with people you know and trust. If you are with people you know and trust and you put your mind to it, you cannot do absolutely anything. I said this to myself and I meant it. But you can do this, Snicket. You can open the hatch and rescue the screaming girl.

But it wasn't the girl who was screaming. The hatch flung open after a long pull, just flung open with a loud, easy *clang* that rang in my ears. It was

244

so quick it was as if the hatch had been joking about being difficult to open. Jake and I looked at each other in astonishment and then scurried through the hatch and down a short metal ladder into a room with a low ceiling and someone screaming in it. The rest of the room was a long laboratory table piled with all sorts of scientific equipment. There were glass tubes and bubbling containers. There were electronic boxes with lights and switches, and blackboards with equations scrawled across them. And there was a girl several years older than I was. She had hair so blond it looked white and glasses that made her eyes look very small. She had a frown on her face, and she was rubbing one of her wrists, which looked swollen and sore. I could see, snaked on the surface of the table, another shackle with the letter C wide open at the end of it. She wasn't looking at me. She was looking into the corner of the room, at the person who was screaming. It was Dr. Flammarion, quivering and stumbling with fear at the girl who was frowning her way toward him. And the girl was Cleo Knight, of course—the real Cleo Knight.

"*Help!*" screamed Dr. Flammarion again. "*Someone help me!*"

Jake hurried to his sweetheart. "Hello, Cleo," he said. "I missed my Miss Knight. I'm glad to see you."

"I'm glad to see you too, Jake," Cleo said, although she hardly looked at him. Her eyes were locked in a glare at the shivering figure of the apothecary. She moved calmly but it was too calmly. "I'm sorry I didn't get in touch with you earlier," she said, in a calm and even voice, "but I was chained up in a basement and forced to continue my experiments. I had it worse than that girl in that book, who goes to live with that family the Reeds, and everyone is cruel to her."

"It's a wonderful book," I couldn't help saying, and I reminded her of the title.

"This guy's named Snicket," Jake said. "He's the one who figured out that you'd been kidnapped, instead of just hiding out like we planned. He's the one who figured out that you were locked up here and made us come and get you." He looked at her wrists and the shackle. "Although it doesn't seem like you needed rescuing, really."

"It was an ordinary enough pin tumbler lock," she said, gesturing to the shackle. "The trick was getting Flammarion to lend me a hairpin. But of course I needed you to come, Jake. I needed someone to open that hatch. And I needed someone to help me take this terrible man to the police."

The building groaned again, and Dr. Flammarion squealed another cry for help, and now Cleo Knight was no longer calm. In two quick steps she tipped over the laboratory table and sent everything crashing to the floor. There was a shattering of glass and the squawking of electrical devices, and a puddle of liquid hissed and steamed on the floor. But Cleo Knight didn't even flinch, a word for the usual reaction people have to a loud noise or an unfortunate event. I didn't know what I had expected to find when I found this brilliant chemist. I suppose I had thought she might be quiet and shy, from all the time she spent in her bedroom working on a formula for invisible ink. But instead she kept walking toward the quivering man in the corner, and pointed a finger at him as furious as the bruise on her wrist.

"You're a monster," she said. It was an angry voice and a quiet voice, and it made me flinch. "You drugged my parents until they couldn't think straight," she said. "You destroyed the note I left for my parents and Zada and Zora. You vandalized my car and lured me into your clutches. You locked me down here and made me work on invisible ink so you could fill this clinic with children and continue your treachery. But that story is over now, Flammarion. You'll never get your hands on my formula, and I'll never rest until Stain'd-by-the-Sea is a proper town again."

When I was eight, one of my instructors took us out to the woods to spend several nights. A friend of mine captured her first bat, and my brother learned how quickly wasps can get angry. But what I gained was a lesson the instructor taught me, that a wild animal, when cornered, may suddenly and desperately defend itself. This is why I try not to spend any more time outdoors than is absolutely necessary. Dr. Flammarion stopped his whimpering and turned around to face all of us, with a wide smile full of unbrushed teeth.

"This story isn't over," he said, and then for some reason he sneered at my muddy shoe. "You have no idea what you've gotten into. You call me a monster, but you have no idea what monsters are coming. You'll never get your hands on Armstrong Feint. You'll never get your hands on Hangfire. And before long we will get our vengeance on your puny, careless town. Now get out of my way. You're just some uppity children, and I'm a fully grown adult with a friend who is good with a knife, and we are miles away from the police or anyone else who can help you."

And then there was the sound of a siren. It was a wonderful sound, over the rain, even though I knew it was not a real siren and not a wonderful person making the sound. It is surprising whom you are happy to see when you are in a basement with a madman. The siren grew louder, and I heard the familiar rattle of the Mitchum station wagon. Cleo grabbed one of Dr. Flammarion's arms, and Jake Hix grabbed the other. They dragged him up the ladder, and I walked behind them. It felt something like a very strange wedding ceremony, and the reception was held in the wrecked dining room, with the wind and rain as guests, the Officers Mitchum as the rabbi, and Stew Mitchum as a sneering flower girl, following his parents through the broken window to behold us.

"What is all this?" Harvey Mitchum asked sternly.

"This," I said, "is Cleo Knight. She had been planning to work in secret on an important formula. And this is Dr. Flammarion, who abducted her so he could get the formula for himself. His accomplice, Nurse Dander, is around here somewhere. She has been provoked and might be dangerous."

Mimi Mitchum peered at Cleo. "Is this true?" she demanded.

"Of course it's true," Cleo said, and gave Flammarion a shove toward the officers. "Nobody would make up something like that."

"In that case," Harvey said sternly to the doctor, "you'll be on the next train to the city, where you will be imprisoned for your crimes."

"My turn," Mimi said sharply.

Her husband frowned at her. "What?"

"It was my turn to give the speech about being on the next train to the city. You got to say it to that Ellington girl."

"Mimi, what difference does it make?"

"If it doesn't make a difference, then—"

A piece of plaster fell from the ceiling to crumble at my feet, and the Colophon Clinic gave another mighty groan, as if it, too, were tired of the Mitchums' bickering.

"Might I suggest we leave?" I said. "This building may very well collapse."

For once the Mitchums did not argue, and soon Dr. Flammarion was the one in chains at last. He glared at the ground. Stew smirked at him. We hurried back through the empty halls of the clinic to the front door. I didn't like the idea that this corrupt doctor would soon be cellmates with Ellington. Except she's not there, I thought. The police were lured away, and Ellington Feint has picked the pin tumbler lock and is out of jail by now. I thought of her running across the lawn, and I thought of the statue she was holding. It will be a while, I guessed to myself, and I guessed correctly. It will be a while before you see her. And indeed my finger was entirely healed the next time I saw Ellington Feint, although I had other troubles.

At the front door it first looked like the Bellerophon brothers were riding a horse, but then I realized that they were sitting on Nurse Dander, Pip on the top half and Squeak on the bottom half, with their hands grabbing her thrashing arms and legs.

"We're happy to see you," Squeak said.

"It looks like you did good work," I told him.

Pip shook his head. "Don't worry about us. Worry about Moxie. She's hurt."

"Bad?"

"If it wasn't bad, I wouldn't mention it." He

nodded toward the far end of the room, and I ran to the girl lying on the floor. Her hat had come off and she was pale, with her eyes closed. There was a long red line down her arm, and it took me a moment to realize that it had been made with Nurse Dander's knife. The weapon lay on the ground, next to Moxie's typewriter. Anyone who thinks the pen is mightier than the sword has not been stabbed with both. I knelt by her and tried not to look at the wound.

"Moxie."

Her eyes fluttered open. "You were right, Snicket," she said, with a smile and then a wince and a frown. "This is dangerous work."

"Does it hurt a lot?"

"That's the wrong question," she said, and closed her eyes again. "The question is, can you save me?"

"This girl needs a hospital," I said to the others.

"This is the only hospital around here,"

Jake Hix said, but Cleo hurried to Moxie and took a look.

"She'll be all right," the chemist said firmly, and in one swift gesture she tore one of the sleeves off her shirt. It was a new shirt, I could tell, one of the many fashionable items worn by the daughter of the wealthiest family in town. Now it was a bandage, and Cleo tied it expertly around Moxie's arm. "See what you can find in those rooms we passed," she said firmly to her sweetheart, and Jake hurried back out of the room.

Moxie opened her eyes. "You're Cleo Knight," she said weakly. "What did Dr. Flammarion want? Who was behind the plot to kidnap you? When will—"

"Shh," Cleo said.

"This is Moxie Mallahan," I explained, "a journalist and an associate of mine."

"I'll answer all your questions, Moxie," Cleo promised, "as soon as we fix up your arm."

There was a rush of cold air, and I saw that

the Officers Mitchum had opened the front doors of the clinic. Stew Mitchum gave me a glare and then skipped down the stairs as perkily as he could. The officers started to follow, lugging Dr. Flammarion and Nurse Dander, who was now also in handcuffs. "Looks like we have the culprit and the accomplice," Harvey Mitchum said to me.

"The real culprit's not here," I said. "Hangfire escaped a little while ago."

"Who's Hangfire?"

"Skip it," I said.

Mimi glared at me. "Don't tell my husband to skip it."

"I can handle this, Mimi."

"Like you handled the drive over here? That was the bumpiest ride of my life!"

"Don't insult my driving!"

"Don't insult me!"

"Could you *please*," Nurse Dander said, "take us to jail now?"

The Mitchums escorted the criminals out the door, and the room was quiet. Pip and Squeak brushed off their clothing and stood up to shake my hand.

"I appreciate your help," I told them, "although I'd like to ask another favor."

"Name it," Pip said.

"In the back of the building is a spiral staircase," I said. "At the top is a room with a broken window, and somewhere in that room is an old-fashioned record player. It was on a bed stand, but Hangfire hid it right before I came in. Please take it, along with all those papers on the desk, to Black Cat Coffee and put it in the attic. There's a cupboard there that's larger than it looks."

Squeak frowned. "Who wants all that stuff? Another associate of yours?"

Moxie opened her eyes and watched me carefully. "I wouldn't call her that," I said, and then Jake Hix came running into the room with an armful of bottles.

"This is all the medicine I could find, Cleo," he said. His sweetheart took the bottles from him, and after quickly examining the labels, she grabbed two and began to mix their contents together. Another piece of plaster fell to the floor, and I was tempted to ask Cleo to hurry, even though she was hurrying.

"Will Moxie be OK?" I asked instead.

"It'll be a few days before she can type," Cleo said, nodding at the typewriter, "but she'll be fine, Snicket. Let me work. I can heal a cut. Chemistry is a branch of science dealing with the basic elementary substances of which all bodies and matter are composed."

"I never found it interesting until now," I said.

"Hopefully, the whole town will find it interesting before long."

"How close are you to finishing the formula?"

"I don't know," Cleo admitted. She peeled back the bandage and began to dab her concoction on Moxie's cut. The journalist winced, and I reached down to hold her other hand. Nobody should feel pain all by themselves. "I thought I was close a few nights ago and tested it out in my bedroom, but it didn't work."

"I know. I tested it myself."

"Well, perhaps my luck will change. I've set up a laboratory in a small cottage right where the sea used to be."

"Handkerchief Heights?"

"That's the one. It's a good location. Some of the ingredients I need can be found near Offshore Island, just a short hike from the cottage."

"Maybe the Coast Guard can help you," I said. "I think they're the ones who ring the bell when it's time to don masks."

"I have a theory," Cleo said, "that the masks aren't for a scientific reason at all. They're just superstition—another fading myth in this town."

"Like the Bombinating Beast," I said.

"Or Colonel Colophon," Jake Hix said. "He was supposed to be a brave war hero, but he turned out to be a villain."

Moxie shook her head. "Hangfire is the villain," she said. "The real Colonel Colophon must be somewhere else."

I opened my mouth and didn't say anything. There was no reason to mention the window in Hangfire's room, which had already been broken, or the swimming pool that churned under it. I just closed my mouth and frowned at Moxie, and Moxie frowned back, and Cleo frowned at Moxie's arm.

"I've got to get that formula finished," she said. "It's a puzzle, but I've got to solve it. Invisible ink that actually works could make Ink Inc. a successful company again. We could save this town from all the people who want to destroy us. I've got to do it myself. I told my mother and father that, in my note. I love them, but my parents have given up on making things better."

"So have mine," Jake said, and the Bellerophon brothers nodded too. Even Moxie nodded in agreement.

"You'll need help," I said.

"I have help," she said, smiling at Jake and then at the entire room. It was the first time I had seen Cleo Knight smile. It was a good smile. I could see why Jake had fallen for the girl who smiled it. Pip and Squeak gave me a wave and left the room to gather Ellington's things, and Jake went to fetch the Dilemma. Everyone had something to do. I started down the steps.

"Where are you going, Snicket?" Moxie's voice was quiet, but I could hear her curiosity. Being curious is the most important part of being a journalist. It might be the most important part of being anything.

"I have a job to do," I said, and I began to walk back to town. Anyone would have given me a ride, but I wanted to walk, so I could think. I had to report to my chaperone, but what, I asked myself, could I report? The building cracked and heaved behind me. Whatever Hangfire was planning, with those tables and fish tanks and shackles for children, he wouldn't be able to do it at the Colophon Clinic. But his treachery wasn't over. It would move somewhere else, somewhere shadowy and hidden, in a town that had more and more abandoned places with every fading minute. It was a puzzle, a dark and lonely one, and if I were a piece in this puzzle, I did not know where I belonged. I needed to put myself aside, just for a little while, until I saw where I might fit in.

CHAPTER THIRTEEN

It was past midnight when I let myself in. For a moment it looked like the Far East Suite was covered in confetti. I could hear Theodora snoring. After all this time it was a familiar sound to me, but I couldn't say that I was used to it. I stepped to the bathroom and turned on the light and left the door open a crack so I could see. The reason it looked like the room was covered in confetti was that it was covered in confetti. There were a few streamers taped to the walls, and I could see a bottle of champagne in a bucket of ice. Theodora was asleep on her bed, with a bright pink party hat tilted on her head. She had fallen asleep in the middle of her celebration for solving the case of Cleo Knight.

I sat on my bed. My feet hurt from the walk back to town. Above me was the usual painting of a little girl holding a dog with a bandaged paw. It had been a long day, and I don't mind saying that I cried a little bit. There is nothing wrong with crying at the end of a long day. I tried to be quiet, but Theodora jerked awake and sat up and looked at me.

"You got your hair cut," she said.

I nodded and wiped my eyes. I'd had my hair cut the last time she saw me. At least she had noticed now.

"Where were you?" she asked. "Visiting your little friend in jail?"

"Ellington's not in jail anymore," I said.

"What?"

"At least, I don't think so."

Theodora stood up from the bed in a cloud of confetti. She took off her hat and threw it to the ground. "This is a disaster," she said. "If the culprit has escaped, then we're failures, Snicket."

"Ellington Feint is not the culprit," I said. "She has nothing to do with the case."

This was almost true, and Theodora almost believed it. "What are we going to do?"

"I already did it," I said. "I'll write up a report in the morning, and you can sign your name to it."

"I'm not sure I like your tone."

"I don't like it either, Theodora. But it's the right tone for someone who has solved the mystery but is still mystified."

"Tell me how you solved the mystery."

I faced my chaperone, S. Theodora Markson.

"Tell me what the *S* stands for," I said.

"Such a tone!" she said, in such a tone. "Not proper, Snicket. Be sensible."

"I'll be sensible later," I said. "Right now I want to get some sleep."

But there was a knock on the door. And then, when nobody answered it, another one. "Mr. Snicket," came the voice of Prosper Lost. "You have a young visitor waiting for you in the lobby."

"Just one minute," I said, and I heard the footsteps of the proprietor pad back down the hall. I looked at the girl in the painting. She was busy with the dog. Theodora glared at me and then lay back down on her bed. In the morning, I knew, I would be responsible for sweeping up the confetti. It was part of my job as an apprentice. It could be anyone, I told myself. There's no reason, walking down the stairs, that you should think it's Ellington Feint waiting for you in the lobby of the Lost Arms.

Sure enough, standing in the middle of the room, just under the statue of the armless woman, was somebody else.

"It's not your fault, Snicket," he told me right away. He'd always had a philosophy that you should not hesitate.

"What is it?" I asked him.

"Can we talk here?"

"No," I said. I knew without looking that Prosper Lost was close by with his ear to the ground, a phrase which here means "his ear to our conversation."

"Can we take a walk, then?"

I nodded. My feet ached. The day wasn't over yet, not even after midnight. I followed my associate out of the hotel and down the street. Naturally, we walked toward the library, though we stopped in the middle of the lawn, where the ruined statue glinted in the moonlight. I could see lights on in the police station, where the Officers Mitchum were arguing over whose fault it was that Ellington had slipped out of the cell, while Dr. Flammarion and Nurse Dander sat, handcuffed and forced to listen. The library looked closed and locked up, although I thought I saw a few moths fluttering near the entrance, now that their home, a tall, broad tree, was gone. I wondered if Dashiell Qwerty had finished all the work he was doing in the library. Perhaps he was sleeping there now. "What happened?" I asked finally.

"Kit's been arrested," my associate said. "My sources tell me they got her just as she was trying to open the hatch. It was too heavy for her to open by herself."

I closed my eyes. It was even darker that way. "She was not supposed to be by herself," I said.

"Snicket, I said before, it's not your fault."

"You can say it as many times as you want."

"Kit knew you wouldn't be there. She

decided to try anyway. And I can't blame her. The Museum of Items hasn't had an exhibit like that in years."

"Eighty-four years," I said. "If we don't get the item now, we won't have another opportunity in our lifetimes."

"She got the item, but she got arrested too. There will be a trial, Snicket. She may very well go to prison."

"Where is the item now?"

"Nobody knows."

"We've got to find out."

"Aye," my associate said with a slow nod. It was his way of saying yes. "You know I'd help you if I could. But I told Headquarters that I had to explore this area. When they find out there's no more water here, they'll confiscate my submarine."

"You'll get it back."

"Not soon enough."

"You shouldn't have come, I guess."

"I wanted you to know, Snicket. Your sister put her mind to it, but she couldn't open the hatch to get out of the museum."

"Thank you," I said, "for telling me."

"You know I'd help you if I could," he said again.

I leaned against the statue and took off my shoe. "Then tell me if you know what this is," I said.

"It's your shoe."

"No, the muddy stuff on it."

"Mud? Moss?"

"It's something else, I think."

Widdershins frowned, and took the shoe from me. He sniffed at it. "Fishy," he said.

"Yes."

"We have it as a snack on board the submarine sometimes. Caviar. Fish eggs. Gustav loves the stuff."

"Thanks," I said, and put my shoe back on.

"Is this part of the case you're working on?"

"It might be."

"What's happening in this town, Snicket?"

"There's a villain named Hangfire," I said. "He kidnapped a naturalist and forced the naturalist's daughter to steal a statue of a mythological beast. He had a chemist abducted so he could steal her formula for invisible ink. He's part of a group of people called the Inhumane Society, and they're planning more treachery. He was last seen pretending to be a war hero named Colonel Colophon, who was injured during an explosion that turned this statue into a lump of metal, and he's planning on capturing a number of children for some terrible purpose."

My associate tapped his finger on the remains of the statue and then nodded at me. "How much of this does your chaperone know?"

"How much does your chaperone know," I asked, "about your secret trip here?"

He smiled at me. "You can't tell them *every-thing*," he said. "They wouldn't understand."

"Who taught you that?"

"You did, Snicket. Remember? You said we could make our organization greater than ever, but only if we stopped listening to our instructors and found new ways to fix the world. It was quite a speech you gave. It almost got you thrown out for good."

"Maybe they should have thrown me out. In Stain'd-by-the-Sea the world looks harder to fix."

"Remember what our associate said," my associate reminded me. "No reality has the power to dispel a dream."

"Hangfire is dreaming up something awful," I said, "and I don't know how to stop him. I don't even know where to begin."

A bell rang then, the clanging alarm from the tower. I pictured the Wade Academy, abandoned on Offshore Island, where Cleo Knight's secret ingredient could be found.

"I heard about this," Widdershins said. "Do we have to put masks on?"

"I don't know," I said. "It might be a superstition."

"How can you be certain?"

I sighed. "I'm scarcely certain of anything, Widdershins."

Widdershins gave me one last nod. "That sounds like apprenticeship to me," he said. "None of us are certain of anything." He waved and began to walk away. He couldn't stay. I watched him go, and then I climbed up to the top of the ruined sculpture. The shape of the lump of metal made it a difficult climb, but at the top there was enough room to lie down and look at the sky. The metal was cold beneath me, but it was better than the bed in the Far East Suite, with the ruins of a wrong celebration. I don't know what I thought of, lying there. I thought of the silver mask, and the face of the Bombinating Beast. I thought of the bandages covering Hangfire's face and the ones around Moxie's wound. I thought about the smell of laudanum, and the mud on my shoe. I thought about the hatch at the clinic and the hatch at the museum and the initials etched into the metal on both of them. I thought about Ellington Feint and her smile, the smile that could have meant anything. I looked at the sky. "No reality has the power to dispel a dream" means that no matter what happens in the world, you can keep thinking about something, particularly if it's something you like.

I lay on the statue and thought, and the world went on without me. Moxie Mallahan was tucked into her bed, and Cleo Knight let herself into Handkerchief Heights, where her scientific equipment waited for her. Jake Hix started cooking up breakfast at Hungry's, and the Bellerophon brothers put an old-fashioned record player and a huge stack of papers in the attic of Black Cat Coffee. S. Theodora Markson slept, and the Officers Mitchum bickered. Ignatius and Doretta Knight received news that their daughter was safe, and Zada and Zora celebrated with something delicious, and Polly Partial discovered that two honeydew melons had been returned to her establishment, while Dr. Flammarion and Nurse Dander sat handcuffed and waiting for a train that would rattle across bridges that were no longer over water, to the city where I no longer worked. And of course Hangfire lurked wherever he was lurking, and Ellington Feint hid wherever she was hiding, and the Bombinating Beast stared out at the world with its empty and evil eyes. All this happened without me, while I watched the night until I'd had enough, and I slid off the statue and got to my feet. I headed toward the Lost Arms and our next case. The bell rang again, signaling the all-clear. I didn't know where I fit in, but I had an occupation. I wasn't certain of anything, but I had a job to do.